MW01611142

RESCUING REX (SPECIAL FORCES: OPERATION ALPHA)

FOB NIGHSHADE

BOOK TWO

JM MADDEN

Dear Readers,

Welcome to the Special Forces: Operation Alpha Fan-Fiction world!

If you are new to this amazing world, in a nutshell the author wrote a story using one or more of my characters in it. Sometimes that character has a major role in the story, and other times they are only mentioned briefly. This is perfectly legal and allowable because they are going through Aces Press to publish the story.

This book is entirely the work of the author who wrote it. While I might have assisted with brainstorming and other ideas about which of my characters to use, I didn't have any part in the process or writing or editing the story.

I'm proud and excited that so many authors loved my characters enough that they wanted to write them into their own story. Thank you for supporting them, and me!

READ ON!
Xoxo
Susan Stoker

AUTHOR NOTE AND TRIGGER WARNING

A lot of very bad things happened in the war in Afghanistan and Iraq. Some things we heard about and some we didn't.

There is sexual abuse in this book, as well as attempted sexual abuse. If that is a trigger for you, please be warned.

I write about these issues because they're important, and people still struggle with them today. Even if you don't have a veteran in your family, maybe you can be more aware socially. Veterans are everywhere, and they deserve our respect and compassion. Most of us couldn't do what they've done for our country.

And as always, I hope you enjoy the book!

Jen

PROLOGUE

PROLOGUE

2nd Lt. Rex Neptune - Afghanistan- July 2012

REX WENT STILL as the dust settled around him. That one had been way too close. What the hell were they doing out there?

The explosions had been coming more and more frequently, which correlated to more injured. They had so many guys already waiting for care, it wasn't even funny. His bladder had been about to burst, though, and he'd had to take a minute for himself. It gave him a chance to look around and see what they were up against.

FOB Nightshade was under attack. Not the regular, semi-random strafing runs the Taliban liked to do. No, this was a full-focus barrage of bullets and explosives. It was the hardest attack they'd taken since he'd been here.

His nerves were shot. Usually, he could roll with just about anything, and more often than not, other nurses came to him for consolation. Physically, he was a big dude, and he knew that made people feel protected, especially in this setting. Nothing really ruffled his feathers, and his patients responded to the laid-back way he had of doing things. So, he did his best to stay calm in all situations. Other RNs called him for backup all the time when they had unruly or just difficult patients.

The constant thrumming of the explosions that rattled the tents, and the responding machine gun fire, had set his nerves on edge days ago. He couldn't sleep, even with the earplugs in his ears 24-7. The canals were sore from being plugged for so long.

It wasn't helping his anxiety. Nothing did. He'd even resorted to sedatives off-shift, just to get some sleep, but he woke up feeling like he'd been drugged, which was worse. He couldn't operate on two hours of bad sleep at night. Not in this environment.

His team had at least another few weeks here,

assuming they weren't overrun. Nightshade was off the beaten track, and isolated. They didn't get the same monitoring as a lot of the other bases. They were well-equipped with several Marine platoons, but that didn't guarantee their safety.

A large explosion detonated just outside the tent. Was that inside the Hesco Bastions? Or had it taken them out? Marines were running everywhere, and his gut was churning. Something was up. Today was different.

The thought had no sooner crossed his mind than another bomb exploded directly behind him, in the recovery tent. The blast sent him spinning to the floor, narrowly dodging another injured patient waiting in the hall. It took him precious seconds to get his breath before he was lurching to his feet. There were so many men stacked in that tent, recovering from surgery. He pushed through the doors and stopped, unable to believe what he was seeing.

Men were on fire. The tent structure had collapsed, and the back corner of the roof was completely engulfed in flames. Rex lunged forward, desperate to pull men out of the fire. Snatching a blanket from the floor, he went to one man and smothered him with the blanket, praying it didn't set on fire as well. Then he unlocked the gurney and shoved it toward the fire-free hallway.

Other nurses were running in now, their faces horrified at seeing the burning men.

"Turn off the oxygen!" Olivia screamed.

He lunged for the next patient burning on a gurney. He remembered this guy. Ryan Dickson. He had a ventilator tube in, and he was beginning to rouse from the sedative. The surge of adrenalin had obviously been enough to wake him. Rex shoved some debris from his body and reached for a bag. He'd have to ventilate for him because the oxygen was off. He attached the bag to the mouthpiece and began squeezing with one hand while unlocking the wheels of the gurney with his foot. He needed to get him out of here.

Ryan tried to take matters into his own hands. Literally. He began to thrash, grabbing at the mouthpiece and trying to remove the tube from his throat. Rex needed more hands.

"Olivia," he yelled.

His manager looked over and understood the situation immediately. Baylee took her patient and waved Olivia to Rex.

"His name is Ryan Dickson," Rex gasped, trying to do everything.

Olivia leaned over the man, looking him in the eye. "Okay, Ryan, we're going to get this tube out, okay?"

The patient seemed to hear her words, and he settled down. They removed the tube from his throat, then waited to make sure he was breathing okay on his own. He seemed to be okay. "Thanks, Liv."

She nodded, then turned to help other patients.

Several of the men now had new burns to contend with in their recovery, but they hadn't lost any of them in the blast. Rex moved from patient to patient, trying to keep them as comfortable as possible, and when things settled down a bit, he sank into an office chair and rested his head on his hand. Within seconds, he had dozed off, exhausted, lulled to sleep by the unnatural quiet.

* * *

REX JERKED awake as an explosion rent the air, followed by machine gun fire that was way too close for comfort. More gunfire responded, and it sounded like it was right outside. Had the Taliban broken through?

Pushing up from the chair, he stretched, back

cracking, and went to the door of the surgical building. Marines were running helter-skelter, not looking where they were going in an effort to get away from the group racing after them.

The Taliban had broken through.

Even as the words went through his mind, men in native clothing slammed through the doors of the hospital, firing wildly. Rex was stunned and couldn't move as he watched patients on gurneys be slaughtered, men he'd worked on and joked with and saved. Blood coated the walls, and he just stood there. Then one of the weapons turned his way, and he knew he was going to die.

The man did not shoot him, though. He started yelling at him in Pashti, motioning for him to move with the barrel of his weapon. Rex took a staggering step and tripped, landing hard against a gurney. Ryan Dickson's bloody face looked back at him, the light fading from his eyes as he bled out.

Fury rose in Rex, and he spun on the attacker, but the man was quicker, expecting retaliation. The rifle barrel swung in his direction, and he saw the man's finger tighten on the trigger. Rex lifted his hands as he gritted his teeth. The man shifted forward and plowed the rifle butt into his jaw, knocking his ass out.

. . .

REX ROUSED as he was being dragged into a room. He kicked out, but the man had already dropped his leg. He danced away from Rex's kick, grinning, and leveled the rifle on him.

Jaw aching, he sat up, wiping the blood from his chin, and he saw the destruction around him. Bodies had been shoved into a pile, heaped on one another ignominiously. It was a horrifying sight, and for a moment, his eyes burned with angry heat. There was a moan from somewhere and one of the Taliban turned, firing his weapon into the pile. The moaning stopped. The sheer cold-bloodedness of the situation was surreal.

"You are medical, yes?" A man asked him, stepping into his line of sight.

Rex looked up. The guy could have been one of their interpreters. Jeans and a cream linen shirt. Boots. Dark hair and eyes. And he spoke perfect British English.

"Yes," Rex said, jaw throbbing with pain.

"A doctor?"

"No. I'm a nurse."

The man frowned and chuckled. He turned slightly to his men and muttered a few words. The men began to laugh, and Rex knew they were laughing at his choice of profession. Whatever. He'd heard it before.

"Why are you doing this?" he asked, motioning with his hand. "These men were already injured."

The English-speaking man shrugged. "They should not be in our country. So, we are moving to take it back. All across the country right now, other attacks are taking place. We will get rid of you American infestation, one way or another."

They had staged this and been building to it. That was why the attacks had been getting more severe. More wounded Marines, more deaths. It had all been their plan.

Rex looked around. It appeared they were keeping the medical personnel alive for now. Rune was here, and Santana. Silvia and another nurse he didn't know well. Maybe if they hung on long enough, they would get reinforcements. He knew Colonel Trent had radioed for support. They were so far out, though…

In his mind, Rex prepared for his own death.

The Taliban moved into an adjoining tent, leaving two guards to watch over them. Almost immediately, Rex heard men being beaten. And laughter. And gunshots.

Twice they brought in Marines to be patched up and cleaned up before they were taken back out. Rex wasn't even sure why they were bothering because, as soon as they left the room, he could hear them being beaten again. Eventually, they would hear a gunshot, and the Marine would not come back.

Rex wasn't sure what they were trying to figure out — numbers on base or their orders — but the Taliban never seemed satisfied. They kept terrorizing people, then shooting them.

One of the Taliban grabbed Silvia Chen by the hair, jerking her to her feet. Rex tensed, wondering if it would make any difference if he tried to intervene. He and Silvia had had friendly relations over the past few weeks, and he genuinely liked her work ethic. She was a strong nurse, and she had a great sense of humor. The woman was tiny, though, and he'd seen the men making motions to her. When the leader of the group went into the other tent, two of the guards jerked Silvia to her feet. The man holding her leaned in to whisper something in her ear, and Silvia paled. Rex glanced around. This might be the only chance they had to fight back in any way. There were the three guards total, and eight prisoners, none of which had any kind of weapon. The Marines were all outside or all dead.

The man punched Silvia suddenly, and Rex lunged to his feet. Immediately, the guy that had popped him in the jaw swung his rifle around. He muttered a few words about this one being trouble, and the gun went off. Rex hissed as a bullet struck him through the shoulder.

"You son of a goat fucker," he yelled, lunging toward the man. Another shot rang out, and he went down hard, pain screaming through his left thigh. It felt like he'd been hit by a Mack truck. Hands were on him within seconds, trying to staunch the blood as well as hold him down.

"He needs medical care," one young orderly in a t-shirt and shorts said, standing up to the guards.

A bullet took the young soldier through the heart.

If Rex could have been more shocked, he didn't know how. One second, the Marine was leaning over him. The next, he was on the floor five feet away, gasping his last breath.

Blinking, he tried to make sense of how everything had gone wrong so quickly. Pressing his hand to his thigh, he tried to stop the leak, but it was an impressive hole, if he did say so himself. His energy began to flag.

The same Taliban that had shot him reached out

and gripped his arm, pulling him to his feet. Pain roared through him, and it was all he could do to stay conscious. Jerking and shoving, the guy took him to an adjoining tent. Rex thought he was about to die, and he struggled.

The man muttered something and shoved him into the room. Rex landed on the bloody floor and yelled out in pain. Then Olivia and Baylee were there. They took him from the man and guided him to the gurney.

"I'm glad to see you alive, Rex. What's going on?" Olivia whispered.

Rex wanted to sag with relief against them, but he didn't dare. His emotions were chaotic enough. He drew in a deep breath and tried to control the pain.

He told them what he'd gathered about the attack, even as they injected him with antibiotics and patched him up. There was no pain medication, which he sorely needed, but Olivia did the best she could as she extracted the bullet from his leg with a set of forceps. Then they sutured everything together. Rex blacked out from the pain at one point, then roused when they were bandaging him. The girls did everything they could for him. As soon as he sat up, the waiting guards took him back to the tent he'd been in with the other prisoners and dropped him against a wall.

They started torturing Colonel Trent next, and it was bad. The man was a hardass, but they very methodically broke him. Then they shot him. Two of the men hauled him next door to Baylee and Olivia to get fixed, but Rex could tell when they dragged him back through that Trent was not much longer for this world.

Rex lost consciousness at one point, and he knew that they weren't going to make it out alive. Silvia couldn't handle the stress and lost it, screaming and crying, scratching her own skin. They put a bullet through her head. Rex was numb to what they were doing. The Taliban would shoot prisoners and one of the medical personnel would patch them up to be interrogated more. It was a demoralizing process. People were dying faster than they could patch them up.

Rex didn't know what to do. They were outmanned and outgunned. And he was injured badly enough that he doubted he could do much anyway.

Two of the guards kept looking at him and motioning to him. One was the asshole who had shot him. The English-speaking rebel in charge was in another room, and Rex could hear the muffled sounds of fists thumping into flesh. They were beating a man for no reason.

Then, into the silence, he heard Baylee yell out. She sounded pissed, which he'd never heard before. Then her voice changed, fear creeping in. She screamed 'no', and he had a feeling he knew what was happening. Then he heard Olivia scream out in a way he'd never heard before, and he had to move. He pushed up from the floor and hobbled toward the room where his team was, ignoring the guards on him. If they killed him trying to save his friends, he would be okay with that.

They let him get to the doorway and see Baylee being attacked, her pants ripped down her legs, before they hit him in the kidney with the rifle butt. As he dropped to the floor, he saw Olivia unconscious on the floor, her leg bent at an unnatural angle and her head bleeding. She had tried to stop them. His eyes went to Baylee. She was fighting like a hellcat, but two men were holding her face down on a gurney. A third was behind her, unfastening his pants, and he knew what was about to happen. Rex tried to push up from the floor, but something struck his head, and the world swam.

When he roused, his upper body was strapped

face down to a bloody gurney. His shoulder screamed with pain, and he felt fresh blood drip down his arm. The stitches had been ripped out. He blinked blood from his eyes. They'd used the straps of the gurney to tie him to it, his arms stretched the length of the gurney. His legs hung heavy, and he used his good one to try to stand. That was when he realized his feet were tangled. And had he been cut on his hips? There was blazing pain, there.

He felt the brush of something sharp against his bare ass, and icy fear rolled down his spine.

He blinked to clear his vision, and he could see he was in one of the surgeries. He couldn't see anyone else, and he glanced around, trying to see who was touching him. It was the Taliban soldier that had been watching him. Apparently, he'd moved him when he was unconscious.

Another man entered the room, grinning a gap-toothed smile, and Rex flexed, gritting his teeth.

The man behind him leaned close, and Rex would have recoiled if he'd had the room. The man's tobacco laden breath rolled over him as he spoke Pashti. Rex thought he recognized 'ass', but nothing else made sense. Then he heard the word *bachas*, and his heart stopped. He had the ass of a *bacha*. That's what the man had said. Rough fingers danced lightly down his ass cheek, and Rex kicked out. Pain roared through his shoulder, and he realized the man had tied his arms to his legs under the gurney. When he kicked out, he ripped at his own injured shoulder.

He didn't care, though. He knew about *bachas* in the country. They were young boys used for sexual services by the Taliban leaders. It was an abhorrent practice that the Taliban relished in, and that the American forces had been ordered to ignore. The American military considered it CSRV, combat-related sexual violence, and they were not allowed under any circumstances to interfere, even when they observed it happening. The practice sickened Rex, because it was young men who were already disadvantaged by the war and their circumstances.

"You son of a bitch. I'm going to kill you," he growled, his body tense. He pulled at his restraints, and the one around his right hand seemed to loosen a bit.

"You're a long way from home, American, and there is no one here to save you," the man whispered in almost perfect English.

That made Rex pause for a split second. Had the guy been an interpreter or something? That English was too perfect. "I don't need someone to save me," he growled, wrenching at his right arm.

Almost simultaneously, a bomb went off nearby, rattling the building. The Taliban started yelling to each other, and Rex could tell they were alarmed. Another bomb went off, then another, and the men ran from the room. Rex took the opportunity to wiggle his wrist free of the thick nylon strap. It wasn't made to be tied into a knot, and it loosened easily when he focused on it.

His head swam, and he knew he'd lost a significant amount of blood. But he was free and moving. Blood was flowing from both of his wounds, but he didn't care about that. One-handed, he tried to shimmy his pants up, but they'd been cut on the sides, as well as his underwear. He realized then that his skin had also been cut and was flowing with blood.

"Fuck," he growled, feeling supremely exposed.

He looked around for anything he could wrap around himself, but there was nothing close. Across the room was the linen closet. If he could make it there, he would find something.

Another explosion rocked the building, and he realized how crazy it was that he was more concerned with covering himself than taking cover. For a moment, he just sat on the cold floor, feeling the blood flow from his body and realizing what a close call he'd just had. Even if he died in the next minute, he would be okay with it, because he hadn't been raped.

What the ever-loving fuck...

Then his mind flashed back to Baylee, and he prayed she'd been able to get away. Or fight them off. She was a strong woman. But he needed to check on them both. With that thought in mind, he looked for a way to get up. There was an IV pole lying beside him. If he could lock the wheels, maybe he could use it for leverage to get up.

Before he could do that, a massive soldier burst into the room, gun first. Rex went still, but the guy seemed to be American. American uniform, Colt M4A1, which the Special Forces preferred. "Fuck, yeah!" he cried, pumping his fist.

The operative held a hand out in a placating measure. "Stay down. It's not secure yet."

Rex stayed where he was, holding a hand to his junk. He looked for anything to cover up with, reaching till he cried out in pain for a tray from a rolling instrument cart. It wasn't much, but it was better than nothing.

He waited, breath held and bleeding, as the American forces swept through the hospital. He could hear weapon fire inside and outside, but it quickly came to a stop. Had they won? Or the Taliban? Was he going to die sitting here on the floor bleeding to death, naked? His heart beat so fast, he thought he might stroke out. Still, he waited, knowing he couldn't get up without help.

As if he'd heard him, the big guy that had come in first entered the surgery. He still had his M4 at the low-ready, but he set the safety and let it hang after he'd cleared the room. Then he came to Rex.

There was a terrible scar down the left side of the guy's face, down to his lips, and Rex fought not to wince in shared pain. But the operator's eyes were clear and direct, and there was a hint of a smile on his twisted mouth.

Rex considered himself a man's man, but he blushed like a schoolgirl when the guy helped him to his feet and his scrub pants fell the rest of the way down around his ankles. The operative righted the IV pole and made sure Rex had a grip on it before he bent down and cut the scraps of fabric away from his feet.

"Are there scrubs around?" he asked when he stood.

Rex glanced around, figuring out which room he was in. "Across the hall."

Without a word, the guy left, leaving Rex bare ass

naked in the middle of the surgery. He came back within seconds, though, dropping a fresh pair of pants open. Matter of factly, he knelt in front of Rex, holding the waistband between his hands.

"My name is Truck," the guy said, voice low. "I'm a combat medic. Before we pull these up, I'm going to have to bandage a couple of places on your hips. Look like knife wounds. They probably need stitches, but we don't have time for that right this second."

Rex stepped into the pants and pulled them up as much as he could, but he could feel the slices on his sides weeping. Obviously, when he'd been unconscious and tied to the gurney, the Taliban had cut his pants off him. And the asshole hadn't cared if Rex got cut as well. He'd probably planned on killing him when he was done anyway. "That's fine."

Rex was amazed at how quickly Truck strapped bandages to his hips and taped them down.

"Are there any other injuries I need to know about?"

Rex knew what he was asking, and he was very glad that Truck was behind him so he couldn't see his face. No eye contact needed. "No, no other injuries."

"Good. These are going to be painful as hell coming off, but I have other patients."

"That's okay," Rex said, feeling the pants slide up over the bandages. He tied the string off and turned to face the man. He held out a hand. "Rex. I'm an RN here at Nightshade."

"Good to meet you, Rex. Now, if you can motor, we have injured."

Yes, he could and would motor.

CHAPTER ONE

Rex was reaching for a plastic cup at the drink station when gunfire ripped through the air, echoing through the convenience store. Immediately, he hit the floor, scrambling for cover at the end of the counter. For a moment, the sound of gunfire from years past echoed through his mind, and he wondered if he had actually heard real gunfire, or if this was some fucked up flashback. He'd had them before, and they could come on suddenly like this.

Then he heard someone yelling. No, they were pleading. It was Mr. Ahmed, who owned the store.

"My son just took the deposit," Ahmed said. "I don't have money in the safe. I will give you what I have in the register."

"Don't lie to me, old man." It was a younger man's voice. Not one Rex knew.

For a moment, he closed his eyes, wondering what he should do. Or if he should do anything. Maybe the kid would just leave if he got the money.

Leaning forward slightly, Rex tried to see what he could see, but he wasn't in a good position. He glanced up at the round security mirror in the corner of the ceiling that housed one of Ahmed's cameras. There they were. Two men, young, judging by their clothes. The one confronting Ahmed was pale skinned, and he held an AR 15 in his arms. The second robber was light-skinned black and held a handgun, though his hands shook around the grip. Both wore face masks and hoodies. And they both struck him as very young.

Rex looked at Ahmed. The old man had his hands up, but Rex could see his anger building. He knew the old guy had a gun under the counter, and if he moved a couple of feet to the right, he would be within reach of it.

Rex took a deep breath, trying to calm the adrenalin coursing through his body. And the fear. He was man enough to admit that this was the closest he'd been to combat in ten years, and the same urge for fight or flight fought within him. Echoes of pain rolled through his body.

Another shot rang through the gas station, into the ceiling tiles. Dust filtered down over Ahmed as he ducked.

"I'm not going to warn you again," the young robber said. "I know what you're trying to do, old man. You need to give me the cash from both registers. And I know you can get in the safe."

Rex drew back, checking his scrubs pocket for his phone. It was in the car. He didn't think he'd need it running in to get a drink and snacks before work, just like he did every other night. This gas station was a half mile from the hospital, and the closest and easiest to pull into.

He wondered if Ahmed had been able to set off an alarm or anything.

Rex glanced around, looking for a way out or a weapon, or something. He hated just sitting here, waiting. His leg twinged from being in the weird position, and he thought it was ironic. He was in a gunfight situation and his thigh was hurting from an old gunshot wound.

Ahmed murmured something softly to the forward kid, but he shook his head, anger radiating from him. "Man, you ain't got no idea. Give me the fucking money!"

"The safe is empty. It's late. The deposit has already gone."

Some instinct told Rex that the boy would not accept that answer. Gunfire rang out, and Ahmed gave a cry.

That obviously hadn't been part of the plan, because the second assailant gasped, his gun hand falling. "What did you do?"

Ahmed had fallen behind the counter. The lead man jumped the counter, setting his weapon down, and started punching buttons on the register. Obviously, he wasn't hitting the right buttons, because the register stayed closed and the boy's anger mounted. Rex eased back behind the counter, wishing he had some kind of weapon in his hand. It had been years since he'd gone through basic, but he could figure it out. The AR the kid carried had been similar to what he'd been issued in the Army. He looked around, searching for any kind of weapon. There was a mop in the corner across from him.

He wondered if Ahmed was dead or just injured. Where had he been shot?

"How do I open this, fucker?" the shooter yelled at the floor. From Rex's position, he couldn't see

Ahmed, but he must have been alive if the kid was screaming at him.

"We have to get out of here, Chu," the second kid said, moving toward the doors. "This isn't what I signed up for."

Then he disappeared through the front door, leaving his buddy behind. Rex would have laughed if the situation hadn't been so dire. Ahmed was probably seriously wounded.

Finally, the shooter seemed to find the button to open the register. The drawer clanged open and he started grabbing money, stuffing it in his sweatshirt front pocket. Rex watched every move he made. The gun was still within his reach. Hopefully, the kid would grab the money and go, letting Rex get to the station owner.

Then the kid glanced up, directly into the mirror in the corner. Rex drew back behind the counter, but he thought he'd been spotted. His heart galloped, and he looked around for any escape. Anything. There was a door to his back, but he did not know if it was unlocked or where it led. Theoretically, it went out the back. Or maybe to the restrooms. He tensed, preparing to bolt. Or preparing to grab the mop. Did he seriously think he could take on an AR15 with a mop?

Rex heard a thump on the other side of the room, and he had a feeling the kid had just jumped the counter again. Now, was he taking off with his loot? Or look for witnesses to get rid of?

Rex knew if he stuck his head out, the kid would see him, but he had to know. He wasn't going to sit here like a fucking duck. He peered out from the corner of the counter.

The shooter was less than ten feet away. Gunfire screamed out again and Rex lunged across the small space, grabbing the mop. He surged to his feet and swung. The mop head was heavy with moisture, and it gave a satisfying thump as it hit the kid in the face, knocking him down. The kid scrambled back, blue eyes wide and dazed behind the off-kilter mask. Rex didn't give him time to snatch up the AR. He kicked it out of the kid's reach and it skittered behind him, toward the drink coolers.

For a long moment, the kid just stared at him, then he leaped to his feet and ran out the door.

Pain blazed across Rex's middle, and he looked down. Apparently, the kid had nicked him. Then his eyes flooded with blood, and he realized he'd been grazed by a bullet to the head. What... the... fuck...

Everything went silent.

Blood continued to pour down his face, but he

gave himself a microsecond to breathe through what had happened. His heart was racing, and he couldn't remember being that scared for a long time. The last time had been ten years ago, almost to the day, during the Rebellion when Nightshade had been attacked.

He blinked his vision clear. Head wounds always bled a ridiculous amount, but he needed to get it staunched. Using his fingers, he tried to find the graze. There. Just on the edge of his temple. A quarter inch deeper and he would have been down.

Ripping his T-shirt over his head, he tore it in strips. He wrapped one around his head and tied it off. With one ear, he listened for movement outside, but he didn't hear anything. It had been almost a minute now. Surely the shooter had taken off?

There was a flash of brake lights outside moving away.

Rex blinked, his head swimming. His gut was beginning to hurt as well, now that he was moving.

Rushing to the front of the store, he went behind the counter. Ahmed was lying in a pool of blood, his hands over his middle. Despite the pain beginning to build in his own body, Rex kneeled down beside the man to evaluate him.

It was bad. Really bad. Blood was flowing freely

onto the floor. Rex scanned the area behind the counter and grabbed a sweatshirt from the back counter. He pressed it to the wound, but he knew the ambulance needed called. He looked around for a phone. There was a cordless on the back counter. It had been under the sweatshirt. Rex snatched up the receiver and pressed buttons. His fingers were slippery with blood, but he managed to get the right ones in.

"911, what is your emergency?"

As quickly as he could, Rex related what had happened and the condition of the patient. Ahmed had slipped into unconsciousness from blood loss, and he knew it would not be a good outcome if he didn't get help soon.

"We have emergency service en-route. Someone already called it in. Help will be there in just a few minutes."

Good. Rex dropped the phone to the floor, not bothering to hang up. He needed both hands to apply pressure and hold the sweatshirt to Ahmed's gut. He talked to the man, falling into an easy one-sided conversation to fill the silence. Ahmed's color got worse and worse, and his pulse began to fade. Just when he thought all was about to be lost, he heard a siren approaching. Within less than a minute, a police car screeched to a stop outside the door, followed quickly by an ambulance. Two cops came in through the front door, a man and a woman, and they cleared the store, weapons out. Then they waved in the ambulance personnel.

Rex related the details of what he'd done and Ahmed's waning stats. The paramedics worked quickly, starting an IV to push fluids.

"I've got this, sir," the second paramedic said, moving in beside Rex. He was holding wound dressings to pack into the injury and slow the flow of blood. Rex backed out of the way, letting the man work, and he sagged back against the cupboard. His vision hazed out, and for a moment he forgot where he was. The past surged back, rolling over him without mercy. He stared at the men trying to save a life and saw other people, female nurses mostly, working over wounded servicemen. His team had been in the thick of the action in Afghanistan, and they'd lost more men than he could even remember.

He blinked, and when he opened his eyes, there was a woman kneeling in front of him. For a moment, the past and present merged, and she kind of looked like Olivia, then other details sharpened. Her dark uniform, and the badge on her chest. The gold-colored nametag said L. Collins.

"Sir, what can you tell me about what happened?"

Rex blinked, glancing around, getting his bearings. "Two kids. One black, one white. They had ski masks on. AR 15 and a handgun. Didn't see the vehicle."

The woman nodded at him encouragingly, her eyes kind as she smiled slightly. "What else?"

Rex racked his sluggish brain. His head throbbed, and he breathed through the pain. "I think the shooter's name was Chew, or something like that."

"Did you see who shot the owner?"

"Chew, the white kid."

The woman was jotting things down in a little notebook. Rex looked down at her head. She had pretty, honey blond hair, though it was scraped severely back into a bun at the base of her head.

A wave of pain rolled through him, and he clenched his teeth. The woman was looking at him oddly. "Are you okay?" She glanced at the bandage around his head, and it must have been dripping again. "Medics!"

A third paramedic kneeled down beside them. He grinned at Rex, moving carefully as he unpacked supplies from a bag. "I think I need to look under that bandage, sir."

Rex snorted. It had been a while since he'd been called sir. "It's just a graze."

The medic snipped the scraps of t-shirt away from Rex's forehead. Almost immediately, he felt blood begin to trickle from the wound.

"Maybe a little more than a graze," the medic corrected. He set a pad against the wound and began re-wrapping the injury. "You're going to need stitches for that."

Rex grimaced, but that made his head hurt more. "Damn it."

He tried to remember who was in the ED tonight, but it escaped him. It didn't matter.

The female cop leaned in. "Is there anything else you can remember about what happened? Where were you when you were shot at?"

Rex blinked, feeling sluggish. His eyelids felt heavy. The adrenalin was wearing off and the blood loss kicking in. "I was, uh, over at the drinks area. Saw them come in and I took cover. Watched him in the mirror." He waved a hand vaguely in the direction. "But the one kid left. He didn't like what Chew was doing. Then the shooter looked up and saw me watching him. He jumped the counter and came after me. He snapped off a couple of rounds. Got my stomach first. Then my head. I smacked him with the mop," he gestured vaguely behind him. "Got him in the head, which knocked his mask crooked. I kicked the AR away, and he took off. I could see blond hair, blue eyes, and a tattoo on the right side of his neck."

The female cop jotted notes on her little pad, but she kept good eye contact, too. He liked looking at her eyes. They were big and calm in the midst of the chaos boiling around them, a pretty blue-gray. She listened to everything he said and didn't argue or suggest. She just listened completely to his details.

Beside them, the team worked the gurney into the narrow space, and Rex knew he was in the way. He rolled to the side and put a hand down to lift himself up.

"Sir, wait! Let me help you."

The world spun and Rex was helped to a standing position by the female cop. He towered over her, but damn, she was strong. She guided him out from behind the counter and to the far end, where there was a desk and a computer. This was obviously where Ahmed did his books and ordering and the like. The cop guided him into an office chair and stepped back. The medic that had been working on him tsked as he saw fresh blood on the head wound. "We need to get you rolling. You could have a concussion as well."

He disappeared, and Rex watched him go. His mind was moving sluggishly, and he wasn't sure if it was from blood loss or something else. Maybe he needed to go in.

A gurney parked in front of him, and the medic collapsed it into the base, snapping it into position. Rex jumped at the sound, his emotions going into fight or flight again. He must have tensed, because the female cop leaned down to look into his eyes. "You're okay," she murmured. Then she gave him a considering look. "What branch were you in?"

"Army," he said shortly.

She nodded, as if it answered a lot of questions. And maybe it did. Maybe she'd dealt with a lot of guys struggling with PTS. In her line of work, she probably dealt with some serious shit.

Rex didn't like that his nerves and emotions were going so haywire. He used to have flashbacks all the time, but they'd eventually faded away. He hadn't had an honest to goodness flashback in about two years. This wasn't an average night, though.

The first ambulance team was loading Ahmed onto the stretcher. The older man didn't look good. His olive skin had paled out from blood loss, and he was unconscious. Rex liked the man. He always had a smile at the ready and was very appreciative of being in the country after being accepted as a refugee. "He has a son somewhere," Rex murmured. "You should let him know."

The woman nodded. "We already have someone tracking him down."

A second gurney stopped beside them, and Rex slid his gaze that way. He could feel his anxiety ratchet up, and he knew he didn't want to lay down there. "I'm fine," he said, struggling to straighten in the chair.

The cop put a hand on his shoulder. "You've been shot, sir. You have to go to the hospital."

Rex didn't mind her touch on him, which was surprising. Most people's hands on him made him cringe, but he knew that the female cop had his best interests at heart. So, Rex let them move him to the gurney. The problem came when they tried to strap him down.

A gray haze settled over his vision, and he felt like he was looking through smoke. It looked like the day his FOB had been attacked, ten years ago. The Taliban had conducted an organized attack of FOBs all across the country, and Nightshade had been one of the worst. Over forty Marines and Army servicemen were killed, many strapped to gurneys, on their base. *His* base.

Rex fought the hands on him, knowing that he was struggling with a flashback, but unable to help himself. The memory of the pain and trauma from that day had swallowed him under.

Then the hands left, and there was a calm voice telling him everything was okay. That voice got through the pounding madness, and he relaxed enough to take a breath. Eventually, the flashback faded, and he reconnected with his surroundings. He thought he'd been behind the counter with Ahmed, but he was now out in front of one of the drinks coolers. What the hell…

The woman cop stood in front of him, a calm smile on her broad mouth. "There he is," she murmured.

The paramedic hovered beyond her shoulder, a shocked look on his face. Rex cringed. It must have been bad to make a medic look like that. "I'm sorry."

The cop shook her head. "Don't be sorry. Seriously. We moved a little fast, maybe. You don't have to be strapped down."

Rex scrubbed a hand down his face. "I can't be strapped down."

That calm smile again. "Roger that. It's fine. But

we have to get you to the hospital. You're bleeding again."

Rex looked down at himself. Yeah, he was leaking blood everywhere. His scrub pants were trash.

"I can put you on the gurney and not strap you down," the medic said. "But you have to promise me you'll hold on in case we're in a crash or something. It's a bit of a security issue."

The guy was joking, but Rex knew there was truth to the words. "I'll hold on," he promised.

Blood was dripping from his head again, and he knew he needed care. Drawing in a huge breath, he looked toward the overturned gurney. Damn. He'd done that, obviously.

The medic moved to the gurney and flipped it right-side up, then stepped back, leaving Rex plenty of room.

Rex looked down at his feet, telling them he had to move. A hand popped in from the side, strong looking in spite of its small size. She had pretty fingernails, painted a metallic dark pink. The color was startling, and he felt a smile flash over his face.

Without hesitation, he took the hand. The cop had been a steadying influence to him, and he needed every bit of it he could absorb. She guided him to the gurney and stood to the side as he lowered himself to the mattress again. He couldn't lay back just yet, but he could sit here a minute.

The woman squatted in front of him, her leather duty belt creaking, still holding his hand. "Better?" she asked, giving his fingers a squeeze.

Rex nodded, his vision tunneling. "I'm fine. You need to go find the shooter."

But he didn't let go of her hand.

"My department is on the job," she said, voice steady. "We have an idea who it is."

Oh, good. That would ease his mind if they got him off the streets. Reluctantly, he let go of the woman's hand, resting his own on the gurney.

A second medic approached, looking grim faced. He planted his hands on his hips as he surveyed the scene. Rex didn't like him.

"We need to get him on the bus," the man growled.

The second medic waved a hand. "We're just taking a little extra time with a vet," he told the grumpy driver.

The man crossed his arms over his chest, glowering. "We need to speed it up. He's bleeding everywhere."

Rex didn't appreciate the tone, but he really was

bleeding everywhere. He looked at the original medic and nodded.

The man moved in. "Mind if I lift your feet to the gurney?"

Rex shook his head and allowed himself to be helped. Then the two men moved in to get the gurney moving. It was a fairly smooth ride until they got to the ambulance. They almost tipped him over getting him in, and for a moment he wished for the security of a belt, but not really.

The female cop followed along behind, keeping eye contact with him. "You're going to be fine," she promised him.

Rex nodded, even as the ambulance doors slammed, concealing her from him.

CHAPTER TWO

Lauren watched the ambulance pull away and worried about the wounded hero. The guy had stepped in when needed, then gotten shot for his effort.

"I think he'll be alright," Diego murmured, nudging her in the arm.

"I know," she sighed. "Why do the heroes have to pay, though? He was being a good Samaritan."

"That's how it goes, sometimes, kid," Diego said, sighing, turning to walk to their cruiser. "You know that as well as I do."

Yeah, she knew he was right. But she still felt bad for the guy. Maybe she would call in later and see how he did. Rex Neptune. Sounded like a damn basketball player or something. After being on the job for the better part of twelve years and seeing way too many bullet holes, she didn't think the wounds were serious, but she'd been surprised before. As for the gas station owner, well, he was a different story. If he survived, it was only because of Mr. Neptune's actions.

Lauren waited until the detectives arrived, did her pass-on, and left the scene. She had reports upon reports to write before she could head home, and blood all over her from helping the hero. Keegan was going to be mad at her. They were supposed to have breakfast in the morning, and she wasn't sure it was going to happen.

By the time she signed off, it was creeping toward six in the morning, and she was dog-tired. On her drive home, she called the emergency department at Santa Rosa Hospital. She would have called her friend Gen, but she didn't think she was working at the moment.

"Hey, this is Officer Collins with San Antonio PD. We had a couple of shooting victims sent there tonight. Can you update me on their progress?"

"Please hold and I'll transfer you to the shift nurse."

Lauren listened to the terrible hold music for a solid five minutes before her call was answered.

"Who is this and what is your relationship to the patient?" a woman with a harried voice demanded.

"This is Officer Collins with San Antonio PD. We responded to a shooting at a gas station tonight, and I wanted to see if I could learn the status of the victims." She reeled off the names.

There was clattering on the other end of the line, like the woman was typing. "Mr. Ahmed is in surgery as we speak. And Rex will be fine. He's getting stitches and will be staying the night for observation. The stomach wound was a through and through and missed everything important."

Relief flowed through her at the news. Excellent. "Thank you so much, ma'am. You have a good night."

"Officer!"

Lauren paused. "Yes?"

The woman hesitated. "Rex is one of our nurses, and he's playing off the injuries. Can you tell me what happened?"

Lauren snorted. "Well, unofficially, he may have attacked a gunman and saved Mr. Ahmed's life."

The woman sighed on the other end of the line. "Yeah, that's kind of what we figured. That sounds like Rex. He gives everything to his patients. Thank you for letting me know."

"And thank you for letting me know about their status. Have a good night."

Lauren smiled as she turned down her road. Being a cop was a hard job and though things had been traumatic tonight, she hoped they turned out for the good. Rex had been a hero, even though he'd struggled. They hadn't apprehended the assailant yet, but it would happen. Somewhere he would screw up or someone would talk, and they would grab him.

She rolled down the window and inhaled the early morning crispness. It was her favorite time of day, when she'd worked her shift and was on her way home. She had enough seniority to transfer to day shift, but midnight shift suited her personality better. She'd always been a night owl, and night shift on SAPD was action packed. Yes, there were a lot of incidents, which meant a lot of reports, but it felt like she helped more people, too.

She slowed her truck as she pulled into the drive to her house. There was a package at the end of the drive, and she shook her head. Freaking Fed Ex. Why couldn't they bring it down the drive? She'd told them over and over again that the dogs wouldn't bother them. She'd even left it on the customer portal in the special directions area.

Parking on the drive beside the house, she went in through the back gate, then up the deck steps to the French doors. The house was silent, and this was the quietest way to enter. No need to wake Keegan or her mother.

Max, their German Shepherd wandered out from the living room and nosed her hand. She stroked his head for a moment, glad he hadn't barked and woken everyone up. She pulled the door open again and let him outside. He would go find the other dogs and say hello.

Once she closed the door and reset the alarm, she headed upstairs. First thing, shower. She could feel the dried blood on her knees where she'd gone down on the floor beside the victim. Rex. The poor guy had seemed shell-shocked. Maybe he hadn't been out of the Army long. His info said he was thirty-two but hadn't said anything about his military service.

Reaching in, she cranked the shower to almost scalding, letting it warm up, then headed to her closet to strip. Her weapon went into the safe, and she hung her duty belt on the heavy hook inside the door. Then she stripped off the rest of her clothes, tossing them aside. She would change her brass in the morning. She was so tired.

The shower rejuvenated her a little, but only enough to plug in her phone before she crawled into bed. Her head hit the pillow, and a vision of bright Caribbean blue eyes haunted her.

CHAPTER THREE

"Would you give it a rest, already," Rex laughed, but there was an edge to the laughter. They were badgering him again. Yes, he knew they were doing it for his own good, but he didn't feel like dealing with it right now.

Bree crossed her arms as she leaned against the nurse's station counter. "You've been alone as long as I've known you. Are you sure you're not gay?"

Rex sighed, planting his hands on his hips. If he'd gotten a nickel every time someone asked or intimated he was gay, he would be a rich man. Male nurses were few. He understood that, but he still tired of the question. Bree had only been on the floor about six months, and he'd headed off her flirtations several times. She was one of those women, though, that didn't understand a man telling her no. So, she looked for other reasons why.

Rex didn't have the heart to tell her she was a shallow bitch, though he thought it most days he worked with her. Bree was a beautiful woman on the outside. On the inside she was petty and insecure, and she was rude to the patients. More than one had complained to him, and he'd suggested they contact the hospital's customer service line.

It was obvious she'd been talked to. About two months ago, she'd come in and done her job very quietly. Felicity Hill, their supervisor, had told him that Bree had had a disciplinary hearing, and that she needed to amend her attitude. Bree had obviously been humbled. Now, though, her bitchiness was creeping back, and it was going to drive Rex nuts. He was going to say something mean and end up in his own disciplinary panel.

"He's not gay. He just doesn't want to deal with your immature bullshit," Genevieve Frank said, and Rex could have kissed her. Gen had been an RN for going on twenty years. She'd seen and done almost everything, and he would take bets on her rescuing a patient more than most of the doctors that currently worked at Santa Rosa East Hospital.

Gen had been his friend for years, ever since he'd

joined the staff four years ago, and he appreciated her bluntness. She reminded him of Olivia, his lieutenant from the Army. Bree did not appreciate that bluntness, though. Her mouth fell open in outrage, and she stared at Gen, as if waiting for her to take back the words.

Gen merely shrugged. "Tough love, dear. You'd be a good nurse if you weren't such a bitch."

Bree's mouth snapped shut, and she turned and stalked off.

"Oh, Gen," Pam murmured, glancing up from her own charts. "You don't have to be so harsh about it."

Gen shrugged, her dark eyes steady. "She knows she's a bitch. Everyone does. And she gets away with it, at the cost of the patients. It pisses me off."

Yeah, it pissed him off, too.

"I wish she'd learn how to deal with patients from you," she told Rex, planting a hand on her hip. "It was why I wanted her to shadow you this week. Sorry if she made your job more difficult."

Rex sighed, appreciating what she'd wanted. He loved working with patients and helping them through difficult periods in their lives. It fulfilled his own life, making sure others had the best care possible. He had one of the highest satisfaction rates in the hospital, and he was proud of that fact.

"Anyway…" Gen said expansively, and Rex cringed. He hoped they would have forgotten the original topic. "I'm setting you up on a date. It's been three weeks since the shooting, and you've been in a funk. You need to break out of it. I have a fantastic friend I want you to meet. Just dinner and a drink, maybe. No long-term commitments. Believe me, she's as reluctant as you are."

Rex sighed, knowing he was going to give in at some point. Gen had his best interests at heart, and that was the only reason he was even considering this. "Is she an airhead?"

"Absolutely not," Gen said, nudging her glasses up her nose. "She's a divorced single mother, and I love her to pieces. She lives down the road from me, and we ride together sometimes. She's crazy smart and I think she will challenge you."

He gave her a flat look, but Gen only grinned. "Come on. You're a great guy, Rex, and I want you to be happy. And I want her to be happy. I can envision you two together. Really. Her ex was an asshole, and he hurt her, so she's a little gun-shy, but I think you would complement her well."

Rex could tell by the determination in her eyes that she wasn't going to let him go without some agreement. "Fine. Give her my number. Tell her I'm free this Friday night."

Gen grinned, reaching for her phone. "That will be perfect! I know for a fact she's off Fridays."

Rex scowled, feeling like he'd just been pushed off a cliff.

In her defense, Gen had been trying to set him up with this woman for the better part of six months, but he'd resisted. Not for any specific reason. He just... didn't really want to take care of anyone. It was hard enough taking care of himself. Everything in him went to his patients.

The shooting last month had kind of shaken him, though. Yes, he'd been skimmed, but just a few millimeters right or left and he could have been blinded, if not killed. It had made him reevaluate a few things. It had also worsened his anxiety. He'd been fine before the shooting. Now he was on edge and cringing at loud noises. It was like the robbery had awoken his PTSD. For years he'd had it under control. Now it was at the forefront of his mind. And the more he worried about it the worse his anxiety was. It was a vicious cycle.

Maybe the date wouldn't be so bad. He needed something new to focus on.

* * *

REX STARED at the message on his phone screen and tried to decide on an answer. Personnel moved around him, and he knew he needed to put the device away, but he didn't recognize the number.

Are you a football or baseball kind of guy? Tell the truth. This is Gen's friend Lauren, by the way.

He sighed, wondering if she really wanted the truth. *Would my man-card be in danger if I said neither?*

LOL! Nope. Just wondering if I should make reservations at a sports-bar or somewhere else.

No sports bar unless they have fantastic food.

Gotcha! You having a good day today?

Actually, he wasn't. He'd hit the gym after work yesterday, and he'd strained something in his quad. Would she care? *Not bad. Pulled a muscle working out.*

Not an important one, I hope.

Rex burst out laughing. Okay, he hadn't expected that. *Only if I want to walk, I guess.*

Lol

And that was the end of the conversation.

Later that night, though, he got a new message. *How's Hopalong?*

Again, he shook his head, grinning. *Hopping along, thank you for asking. How's your night going?*

Gen had told him they were both working night shifts, so he figured she was at work right now.

Oh, you know. Just the average almost-full-moon night of hookers, thieves and wanna-be cops.

Sounds busy.

Yeah, but I would rather be busy than bored.

Same, he typed out.

Current craziness...

A picture followed, and he couldn't exactly tell what it was. *Are those legs?*

Yup. Homeless dude thought it would be a good idea to sleep in a storm drain. Good thing we haven't had rain recently bc he's stuck. Waiting on the FD.

Rex shook his head and moved to lean against the wall, out of sight of the other staff. *Darwin at work?*

LMFAO! You know, I really think that sometimes! Have a great night! Gotta go!

She texted him several more times over the next few days. Just little things, wondering how he was doing. She wasn't invasive or anything, and he found himself looking forward to her little conversation gambits.

CocoPuffs or shredded wheat?

Shredded wheat bites with the sugar on top. And the more sugar the better, he typed back.

So true!

An hour later he got another message.

Cabin in the woods or shack on the beach?

Depends upon whom I'm with.

Oh, good answer! And a correct use of whom! I'm impressed.

Snorting, he dropped his phone in his pocket and pushed off the wall. He already liked this woman, and he hadn't even met her.

Two more days.

CHAPTER FOUR

Lauren cursed as she caught the next red light, and the one after that. She was running ten minutes late. If she hadn't left early, she would have been late, which she abhorred in a person. She slid into the parking spot three minutes before eight. Just enough time to check her lipstick, fluff her bangs and walk into the restaurant.

It was weird being out of uniform. In an effort to be cooperative, she'd dressed up a little. Meaning she put on nice dark skinny jeans and a pretty blouse, then some dangly silver earrings and a necklace. Her hair was down and curled in long, loose waves. She even added some makeup, more than what she normally wore to work. Gen had come over to critique her before she left.

"Do you even own a dress?" the older woman had asked, one brow lifted as she eyed her critically.

Lauren snorted. "Nope. Not that I would wear one for a man. What a waste that would be. If he doesn't like me in jeans, then what's the point? If I'm not in uniform, this is what I wear."

Gen had sighed. "Yeah, I suppose."

Lauren thought this was a waste of time. Gen had been after her for months, though, and she was tired of dodging. Tired of hearing how great her friend Rex was.

The first time she'd heard the name, Lauren had been jarred. Then the pieces had started to click together. Was this the same Rex that had been in the shooting last month? And had saved Mr. Ahmed's life? Surely, they didn't have two male nurses named Rex on staff at Santa Rosa Hospital?

The fact that she kind of knew the man added a different dynamic to the dinner. She remembered him as being a tall, blood covered mess with nice abs. And pretty, bright blue eyes that seemed haunted with memories. He'd been struggling with past trauma that night. If she was honest with herself, she remembered way more details about the man than she was comfortable with.

The last aspect was a worry. She'd dealt with Post

Traumatic Stress in her last marriage, and it hadn't ended well. Actually, it had been hell on earth for her and her son, and she wasn't sure she wanted to deal with that type of situation again.

Lauren felt bad knocking the man out of the running before they even met. Not that there was anyone else competing, but... she was okay being alone, and running her little family the way it needed to be run. Keegan was more secure now, even though her work sometimes interfered with their routine. But that was when her mother stepped in to cover.

The only good mark on the night was that she knew he was funny, because he'd responded well to her text messages. And after a few days, even he had sent her some funnies. A sense of humor was paramount with her.

Lauren strode up the walkway and into the restaurant. It was one of the best in the area, and regardless of the outcome, she would get a good meal.

Once inside, she surveyed the tables. She didn't notice him right away, so she smiled at the hostess. "I'm meeting someone here," she started.

The girl held up a hand. "Are you Lauren?"

She nodded, a little worried.

"Follow me."

The girl led her through the restaurant and out onto a patio in the back. There were only a few tables back here, and only one was occupied. He must have been watching the door, because he stood as soon as they entered.

Lauren stalled out a little, blinking, as he turned to face her. Holy hell…

The guy cleaned up like a dream. He'd been wounded and blood-soaked, and she hadn't been able to see how handsome he was. And he was tall. At 5' 9", she was a little above average herself, and she really didn't want to deal with any Napoleons. When she'd helped him up at the robbery, she'd been aware that he was rangy and muscular. A cop was always aware of that stuff, because there was always the possibility of having to fight the one you were helping. And she hadn't forgotten the line of abs. But his face… It had been coated in blood at the scene, his dark hair mussed around his head. Now, though, she could see how incredibly handsome he was. Dark brown, curly hair rested just on his collar, and was gelled into place. Some rested over his forehead, covering where she remembered the graze being. His cheeks were lean, and he was clean shaven, highlighting a little divot in his chin. He smiled at her, and lines bracketed his mouth, but his eyes… they lit up. Lauren could see appreciation in his look, and she was a little glad she'd taken some extra time with her appearance.

This isn't going to go anywhere, damn it, she reminded herself ruthlessly.

Boy, he was nice to look at without all the blood, though.

The hostess stopped at his table and dropped off a couple of menus. Lauren didn't even hear her leave, because she was in front of Rex and looking up at him. "It's nice to finally meet you," she said, holding out her hand.

Rex took it, one side of his mouth tipping up. "It's nice to meet you as well. I hope you don't mind being outside."

Lauren looked down at their clasped hands, wondering why she was suddenly overtaken by nerves. Her fingers were wrapped in his warmth, and it was okay. A little better than okay. She pulled her hand back and glanced away before taking her seat. Why did she suddenly have the feeling she was in trouble?

"No, I don't mind being outside," she said.

CHAPTER FIVE

Rex stared at Lauren an embarrassingly long time, but he couldn't help himself. She was stunning. For months he'd scoffed at Gen, arguing against the set-up, but maybe she was onto something.

Lauren was taller than average. Rex thought the top of her head would rest perfectly under his chin. That was a strange thought, because he hadn't desired physical closeness from a woman for a long time. Or maybe he'd just shut down that side of his personality. When people got close, they asked questions.

But her face, and her blue-gray eyes... Why did she look familiar to him?

She must have seen he was trying to tease it out, because she smiled slightly. "Not sure if you remember me, but I responded to the robbery at the Quik Stop."

Her gentle words hit him like a ton of bricks. "You were the cop..."

She smiled again, a little broader this time, and images clicked into place. It had been a chaotic night, but there were flashes of calm, usually when he was looking into her eyes. She'd been completely indefatigable, a harbor in the storm, as he tried to get his bearings.

"That was me," she confirmed. "I didn't realize who you were until I talked to Gen the other day, and she mentioned your name again. There aren't that many male nurses named Rex at Santa Rosa."

He snorted, sinking down into the chair opposite hers. "No, there aren't. I think I can count on one finger how many."

She gave him a broad, knowing smile, and Rex grinned back at her. His mood had shifted. Dread had ridden him for days, but now that he knew who she was, the dread drifted away on the cool evening air. It didn't mean they clicked completely, but she already knew he struggled with posttraumatic stress, which was the biggest hurdle he had in relationships.

And she was a cop, so she understood probably a lot more than the average person did.

Rex realized he was just staring at her, and he looked away. "I'm sorry. Don't mean to make you uncomfortable. You just... whether you realize it or not, you really helped me temper that night. When I think about what might have happened..."

"I think you would have been okay," she said, leaning back in her chair and crossing her forearms over her lap.

Rex shook his head. "No. I've been thinking about it. Worst-case scenario, I would have gotten lost in a flashback when they strapped me down, and I would have ended up in a psych ward somewhere. But you recognized it, didn't you?"

Lauren nodded. "My ex-husband served, and he didn't control it well."

"Hence, the *ex*, I assume," Rex said, carefully.

Nodding, she reached out for the water glass, taking a sip. "And there were other reasons," she said softly.

"This got serious way too fast, didn't it? We haven't even gotten through the basics yet. Hi, I'm Rex Neptune. I'm an RN at Santa Rosa and I like to hike."

Grinning, Lauren reached out and clasped his

offered hand. "Hi Rex. I'm Lauren Collins and I'm an SAPD officer. I have a twelve-year-old son named Keegan and I like to watch trashy reality TV."

They laughed together, and it was strangely easy. A server arrived, offering appetizers, and Rex chose a couple from the menu. Then he sat back and just looked at her. "How long have you been a cop?"

She tilted her head, her long honey colored hair sliding over her shoulder. "Going on twelve years now. "

"That's amazing," he said, shaking his head. "It's a hard job."

She nodded. "Yes, sometimes. It's getting more dangerous, but…" she shrugged. "What can you do? Your job isn't a walk in the park, either. I'm sure you have stories."

Rex snorted. "Oh, I do. And I've been in my share of fights in the hospital, too. I tend to get called when the crazies come in."

"Well," Lauren said, quirking a brow, "look at you. I think you can handle most things that walk through the door."

Rex grinned, and they spent a few minutes comparing crazy suspect/patient stories until the server brought their appetizers. They both reached for food, and it gratified Rex that Lauren was actually eating. He couldn't stand it when women tried to pretend to be something they weren't. He saw it all the time at the gym.

"This is fantastic," he murmured. He'd ordered some kind of stuffed mushroom, and the topping was phenomenal. Crusty and cheesy. "I've never been to this restaurant."

Lauren lifted her brows at him. "You must not be from here, then. This place has been in business a long time. I wasn't sure you'd like it."

Rex tilted his head. "So far, it's fantastic. And no, I'm not from here. I'm originally from Virginia. Most of my family is from the Carolinas. Though we have a few strays in West Virginia and Ohio."

Lauren snorted. "I get the stray thing, but I think I'm the stray. Most of my people are in Montana. They've never understood my need to be in Texas."

Rex couldn't help but grin. "I love Texas. It feeds my soul. I love the expanse of it."

Lauren nodded. "We have a little place outside of town, enough for some critters for the boy. We absolutely love it."

Rex was surprised. She was too put together. He couldn't imagine her mucking stalls or cleaning pens. "Critters, huh? Like dogs and cats?"

Lauren gave a cute little wince. "And a guinea pig, a rabbit, three horses, some chickens, two alpacas…"

Rex blinked. "Damn," he breathed. "Now that's a lot."

"My parents believed in pets for children, and I do as well. I think it makes them more rounded individuals."

"I agree," Rex told her. "I wish more people had had pets as kids. Maybe we wouldn't have so many assholes."

Her head tipped back and she laughed, and Rex felt like he'd won a medal or something. Lauren appeared very collected, and her personality was a little difficult to uncover.

The server arrived then, bringing their entrees. Lauren had ordered a fire-roasted chicken, and he'd ordered a filet. Both plates looked amazing.

"Not gonna lie, my mouth is watering," Rex told her.

"Dig in, then," she told him.

Rex cut into the steak, and it was as good as it looked.

"Not to be too forward but try a piece of the chicken. I haven't used my fork yet."

She ripped a piece of chicken from the bone and

reached across to set it on his plate. Rex blinked, looking down at the piece. It had been a long time since he'd been fed. He popped the piece into his mouth.

"Oh, man," he groaned. "That is so good. The smoke on that is amazing."

Lauren nodded, grinning. "They started from a little roadside stand, selling whole chickens. And they've grown into this." She glanced around the impressive space. "How long have you been in San Antonio?"

He waved a hand. "About four years. I was in Dallas for a while, but I wanted something a little smaller, where I could settle in. I'm also going back to school for another certification."

Her eyes widened. "Oh, really. Because you don't have enough to do."

He shrugged, a little uncomfortable. "I don't have a family, so I might as well."

"So, would that be a doctor of nursing?" she asked.

"Yes, assuming I make it all the way through," he laughed, swallowing a piece of steak. "The classes are tough. And it's been a while since I've been in school."

"Oh, yeah. I don't know if I could do it at my age.

I mean, I take the occasional night course, but there's no way I could go back to full-time school."

Rex shrugged. "I don't have the same responsibilities you do."

They chewed for a minute, enjoying the food. The silence wasn't stilted, though. It was very easy.

"Gen says you're indispensable," Lauren said, shifting gears. "Which is saying a lot. She can't stand most of the people she works with. She also says you're the best nurse she has on her floor. And that you work all the overtime you can. Not for the money, but because you care for your patients."

Rex grinned and shrugged. "I love Gen. She's one of those women that just doesn't give a damn what other people think about her. She'll do what's best for her patients, no matter what."

Lauren took a drink of water. "That's what she said about you, as well. Maybe that's why the two of you get along."

Nodding, he shook his head. "Plus, she already has a partner, so she's not constantly hitting on me. It can get a little awkward being one of the few guys on the floor."

"And I'm sure your looks don't help."

Rex grinned. Yeah, he was handsome, he was aware, but it was nice she pointed it out as well.

Maybe she wasn't as cool as she pretended. He lifted a brow at her. "What about my looks?"

Lauren blinked, then the slightest of flushes pinked her cheeks. "Quit playing, you know you're good looking."

Rex laughed, shrugging lightly. "I've been told a time or two. I just wanted to make you say it."

Lauren rolled her eyes, obviously flustered, and he thought it was one of the cutest things he'd seen in a long time.

LAUREN COULD HAVE CUSSED, but she didn't want to be rude. The guy was flirting with her, and she found she didn't mind it. Yeah, he had a bit of an ego, maybe, but that was okay. He had to be strong to be in the job he was in. *And* he was going to school.

She'd done a few night courses herself, going for a management degree, and it was no fun trying to juggle. She was very fortunate that her mother had moved in with them after the divorce, giving her the option to do what she wanted and needed to do. There were nights she worked until dawn, came home and slept, and got up to do it all over again.

Keegan was her priority, and she tried to be there for his baseball games and other activities, but it was hard. Their household ran on her income. Momma had some money daddy had left, and her social security, but it wasn't much. The Collins family would never be rolling in money.

When Sam had left, he'd taken everything he could. He'd drained their checking account, and the meager savings account she'd started. He'd even taken the money from Keegan's college account, which they'd been stashing bits into for years. It had had the most money in it, and she would never forgive him for doing that to their son.

Luckily, she had several years to make up for the theft.

"What put that dark look on your face?"

Lauren glanced up at the man sitting across from her. Rex differed from Sam in so many ways. Sam had been good-looking, in a guy next door, kind of ordinary. Rex was something incredibly different. He kept his thick, walnut brown hair cut short, but long enough to take advantage of the curls. His face was broad and angular, brows thick over rich electric Caribbean blue eyes. His nose had been broken, and he had a straight-line scar running across the corner of both lips, on the left side. It was a curious mark.

And he had the kind of body that would make

her call for backup before she got into a scrap with him. The guy was about six-two and stacked with muscle. He was a typical romance novel type. Lauren could just imagine her mother's reaction if she ever saw him. Sofia always had romance novels in her hands. Lauren couldn't remember a time when her mother hadn't been reading. She would view Rex as 'swoon-worthy'.

Lauren smiled slightly and looked down at her plate. She didn't have the spare time to read like her mother did, but she recognized handsome when she saw it.

"Ah, nothing you need to hear me complain about. I was just thinking that my mother would love you."

Rex grimaced. "I'm not really in the market for a cougar."

Lauren burst out laughing, covering her mouth. She admired the wit, and he hadn't even hesitated at uttering the comeback. "Oh, you have no idea."

They laughed together, and Lauren wondered if he was funny because she hadn't been entertained for a while, or if she just *thought* he was. Diego, her partner, was funny in a dad-joke kind of way, but he was a dad, and almost old enough to be her father. And that was how he treated her usually. Rex had a flirting kind of humor she didn't realize she'd missed.

There was something in his expression, though… some lingering shadow in his eyes.

Lauren wondered if he felt like he needed to perform or something. His patients probably needed him to be upbeat and fun. Maybe that was his way of getting through life. "No kids or significant others?"

He shook his head, cutting into another piece of steak. "Not that I know of. I was engaged for a while, but we separated a few years ago."

"I'm sorry," she murmured.

Rex shrugged. "It wasn't meant to be."

"How long have you been at Santa Rosa?"

"Four years now. I was in Dallas, but I needed something a little more laid back. Less stressful."

"I can see that," she said softly. "I trained in Dallas, and I didn't like it. Too urban. San Antonio is starting to get that way too, though, with all the growth. I'm not sure I'll be able to go anywhere else, though."

"How far out of town are you?"

"Close enough to be called in when they need extra officers," she laughed. "Which I suppose may be too close."

"Not if you enjoy your job."

Lauren tilted her head. "I do enjoy my job, mostly. It's easier now that my son is a little older. He's twelve, and more self-sufficient. He understands a little better what goes into my job."

"Is it just you and he?"

Lauren shook her head. "Not exactly. My mother lives on the property as well and watches him for me when I'm working."

"Oh," he said, brows raising. "That's convenient, then."

"It is," she agreed. "And you said you were from Virginia?"

He smiled slightly. "Yes."

"Bit of a change from there to here," she murmured.

They compared states for a bit, then his expression shifted.

"So, not to bring the mood down, but did they find Chew?"

Lauren finished her bite and sat back in her chair. "Not yet. We found the accomplice, but he's not talking yet."

"Young black kid?"

She nodded. "He's been in trouble before with this kid, so it's not much of a leap. We just have to wait for him to surface. He doesn't have a great home life, so he'll have to hit the streets before too long."

Rex shook his head. "It's a shame they think that's the way to make a living."

She shrugged a little. "Well, when you're brought up on government assistance and have to support yourself early, you look for the easiest way to do it."

"Yeah."

And he'd seen it in the hospital as well. People coming in for minor things just to get off the streets, especially when it was cold. It was heartbreaking.

"So, what do you like to do for fun," she asked, obviously trying to lighten the mood.

Rex leaned back in his chair. "Well, I have an old Mustang I'm working on restoring. I like losing myself in mindless jobs."

"I get that."

"How about you?"

"Well," she said, smiling. "I'm not very crafty, but I do love my animals. I'll go out and brush on them for hours if I need to relax. We both get the good from it."

"That does sound relaxing," he murmured.

"I tend to find a lot of strays in my job, and some-times I just can't call animal control. I drive my mother nuts."

He chuckled at her shamefaced expression. "I have a feeling you do."

Lauren grinned and shrugged. "She fusses at me for a minute, then she falls in love too. Besides, I get it from her."

Rex shook his head. "Sounds like you live in a zoo. I don't even have a cat. Or dog."

Lauren's brows shot into her hairline. "Seriously? Nothing? I don't think I've ever talked to anyone without a dog or a cat. Which do you prefer?"

"I prefer dogs, but I work a lot. I never felt like it would be fair to an animal to be caged all day while I was at work."

Her expression softened. "Okay, I can agree with you there. Fur therapy is priceless, though. You ought to see if your local animal shelter needs a dog walker or socialization visitor."

"They do that?" he asked curiously.

"Sometimes," she nodded. "They're usually so understaffed they appreciate the help. My son and I have done that a few times. We can't adopt, but we can support them in other ways."

Rex sat back in his chair, mouth quirking. "Sounds like you're building a good foundation with your son."

"Trying," she sighed. "It's difficult competing

against his video games. The boy lives and breathes Minequest."

Rex had heard of the game, but never played it. He must have looked a little clueless, because she pulled something up on her phone. "It's like digital Legos."

"That looks pretty cool, actually," he murmured.

She waffled a hand as she set her phone aside. "It is. Better than a lot of other games. There are so many first-person shooter games, now, it's not even funny."

Rex nodded. They'd had their own issues with video games getting out of hand, and the players picking up real guns. It was stupid and senseless, and he hated that kids were being trained to shoot people.

The server arrived then, asking if they'd like dessert. He looked at Lauren, one brow raised.

She gave him a smile. "I never turn down dessert. I'll do the chocolate cake, please."

Rex chuckled, "I'll have the same."

As they waited for their dessert, Rex's mind wandered to Lauren's son. He couldn't help but wonder what kind of person she was raising. He admired her commitment to helping animals in need and hoped that her son would follow in her footsteps.

Lauren caught his gaze and raised an eyebrow. "What's on your mind?"

Rex hesitated, unsure if he should voice his concerns. He decided to take a chance. "I hope you don't mind me asking, but is everything all right with your son? You seem a little worried."

Lauren sighed, glancing around the restaurant. Then she stared at the tabletop for a moment before lifting her eyes to his. "It's complicated. He's been acting out lately, staying up all night playing video games and talking back some. I'm just worried that I'm not doing enough."

Rex wanted to reach over and take her hand, but he wasn't sure how she'd feel about it. "It sounds like you're doing everything you can. Parenting is never easy, especially when you're doing it alone."

Lauren smiled gratefully at Rex, appreciating his words. "Thank you for saying that. It means a lot."

He reached across and gave her hand a gentle squeeze. "Have you tried talking to him about it? Maybe finding out why he's been acting out?"

"I have," she said with a sigh. "But he's not very forthcoming with information. He just shuts down whenever I try to talk to him about it."

Rex leaned back in his chair, deep in thought. "Well, maybe we can try a different approach. Maybe he needs someone to talk to that isn't his mom. I could talk to him, if you'd like."

Lauren's eyebrows furrowed. "Why would he talk to you?"

Rex shrugged. "I don't know. Maybe he needs someone who can relate to what he's going through. I wasn't exactly a model teenager myself."

Lauren chuckled. "I find that hard to believe."

"Besides, kids like me."

He shrugged his big shoulders, and her eyes followed the movement. Oh, yeah, she could see kids being drawn to him. She definitely was.

CHAPTER SIX

They lingered over dessert. Lauren ate small bites, dragging her spoon lazily through the chocolate sauce. For some reason, the feminine move struck Rex hard, and he wondered if she was doing it deliberately.

No, that was ridiculous. She had no idea what she was doing to him. If she did, she would stop giving him those wide-eyed, appreciative looks every time he moved. It made him want to stand up and rip his shirt in half, or something, to show off for her. For the first time in a long time, he was attracted to a woman.

As they finished their dessert, Rex couldn't help but feel a sense of longing. He wanted to spend more time with Lauren, to get to know her better. But he also knew that he needed to be careful. He couldn't risk ruining their newfound friendship by making a move on her too soon.

They split the tab, which was perfectly fine to Rex. Lauren had set the location up, which he appreciated.

"I don't know that I'm ready to go," he admitted, frowning as he sat back in his chair.

Lauren grinned. "Well, if you want to get out of here, I might know a place…"

"Let's go," Rex said, pushing to his feet.

Lauren giggled, and he thought it was one of the cutest sounds. Rex knew she probably felt too mature to giggle, but that's exactly what it was, and he loved the sound. Resting his hand lightly on her back, he escorted her from the restaurant.

She hesitated in the parking lot. "It's just a block away if you'd prefer to walk."

"That's fine."

Lauren led him down the street and around the corner to a cozy little bar that Rex had never noticed before. It was dimly lit, with a comfortable atmosphere and a live jazz band playing in the background.

Rex couldn't help but feel a sense of relief as they settled into the booth. This was exactly what he needed – a chance to unwind and enjoy the moment. He leaned back in his seat and watched as Lauren tucked her hair behind her ear, a smile playing at the corners of her lips. Lauren pressed a button on the table. Rex was curious, but he didn't question her. She'd done well with the night so far.

The server came to take their order and returned promptly with drinks.

"You know," Lauren said, taking a sip. "I had a great time tonight."

"Me too," Rex replied, taking a sip of his own drink. "You made me laugh with your texts, but that doesn't always translate to in-person."

Lauren nodded, a glint of something in her eyes that Rex couldn't quite decipher. "I know what you mean. I've been fooled before."

She asked about the injury to his stomach, which he assured her was fine. "Good," she said, "because I didn't want you complaining of an injury when I kick your ass in a few minutes."

Rex's brows popped up, and he barked out a laugh. "Just how are you going to kick my ass," he laughed.

"Just wait and see," she murmured.

So, they sat listening to the music and enjoying each other, chatting about inconsequential things.

Then the light at the back of the table turned green. Lauren slid from the booth. "Bring your beer," she told him, heading for a doorway.

They headed down into softly lit darkness. It was just visible enough for him to see the stairs beneath his feet. The room opened up and he realized they were in a second bar. Billiard balls cracked together softly, and he followed along as Lauren led him to a table. They set their beers down and she moved to one of the free tables, racking the balls.

Rex grinned, watching her move. The woman was strong and solid, but not heavy, by any means. She leaned over the table and he couldn't help but trace the line of her body.

Lauren glanced up, and Rex knew he was totally caught. A smile quirked her lips, and she moved toward him. Somewhere she'd picked up a cue stick. She rubbed the tip of the stick with blue chalk as she walked toward him, and Rex felt a rush of heat head south.

She had to know how sexy she was...

"Stripes or colors?" she asked, voice low.

Rex gave her a crooked smile. "Lady's choice."

Lauren stopped right in front of him, and he wondered if he was going to keel over from a heart-attack. Her full breasts were millimeters from his chest, and her mouth was mere inches from his own. Did he dare kiss her?

Leaning up on tip-toe, she pressed a kiss to the dimple in his chin, then turned away. Rex's heart was thumping in his chest. That was the most action he'd seen in a while. Well, other than old lady Baron feeling up his ass the other day.

Being with Lauren didn't make him feel like a fraud. When he was with other women, he forced himself to have a good time. He wasn't forcing himself to do anything tonight. Well, other than keep his hands off of her.

She broke the formation, and several balls went into the pockets. Rex had played pool before, but he wasn't great. He had a feeling he was going to get his butt kicked, as she'd predicted. Maybe he could make it fun, though.

"Loser gets a conciliatory prize," he said, and she tossed him a grin.

"So sure you're going to lose, huh?"

Yeah, he was pretty sure. "Winner gets a prize, too."

"Oh? Like what?"

"A kiss on the pool table."

Her eyes flashed, and she paused long enough to lean against her stick. "And the loser gets...?"

"A kiss on the pool table."

Lauren burst out laughing, shaking her head. Her long golden hair curtained over her shoulder as she turned, but he had seen the flash of awareness in her eyes.

Rex was content to sit on the stool and watch her play. He knew he was getting a kiss either way, so he just watched her. That was when she screwed up. She botched her strike, and the white ball dropped into one of the pockets.

Grinning, Rex pushed up from the stool and stalked toward her. There was a flash of something in her eyes as she waited for him.

Rex couldn't deny the growing attraction he felt for Lauren. He found himself leaning in closer to her, his eyes locked on hers. She seemed to sense his desire, because she leaned in too, her lips parting slightly.

Then he turned away. She wasn't going to get it that easy.

Rex retrieved the ball, positioning it where he wanted it. Lauren was still staring at him, and she hadn't moved. Rex paused in front of her, and her gaze settled on his lips. It took everything in him to refuse to lean down five inches.

"Excuse me," he murmured. "You're blocking my

shot."

Lauren's cheeks flushed a deep pink he could see even in the dimness of the room, and she spun away. She settled over to the stool she'd chosen and tipped her beer bottle back, drinking most of the bottle.

Rex dragged his gaze away and focused on the balls. Obviously, he was stripes. He took a breath and exhaled, aiming down the cue. The first ball went in perfectly, then the second. Lauren's mistake had worked in his favor, because he worked all the way through the table. The last ball fell into the pocket perfectly, and he looked up.

Lauren's lips kicked up at the corner. "I don't usually get beat."

The words were barely out of her mouth before Rex cupped her face in his hands.

They kissed like long-lost lovers, and Rex was stunned at how good she tasted. She should have tasted of beer, and there were hints of it, but that was overwhelmed by a spicy sweetness that made his senses sing. He couldn't get enough of the flavor of her.

Whether or not intentionally, her breasts rubbed against his chest, and he took a minute to look down. She had fantastic breasts, and imagining what they looked like could very likely kill him.

They broke apart, breathing heavily. "Wow," Rex said, his voice hoarse with desire. "I've been wanting to do that all night."

Lauren smiled, a mischievous gleam in her eye. "Me too, actually. I didn't expect it to be that good, though."

Rex grinned, loving her honesty. Then he kissed her again, pulling her body tight to his own. He could feel her heat radiating against him, and it stoked desire. He ran his hands over her curves, pulling her even closer.

Lauren moaned softly, her fingers tangling in his hair. "Rex," she whispered, her lips brushing against his ear. "I'm about to tell you to do something dangerous."

Rex knew what she was going after. They'd known each other mere hours, but they were already thinking about sleeping together. He didn't need any more encouragement.

After he paid the bill, he took Lauren's hand, leading her out of the bar and into the cool night air. They walked back to the restaurant, and Lauren motioned to her blue truck. His own truck was right next to hers. She paused at her driver's side door. "We're a little crazy, aren't we?"

"A bit, yes. We can call it off here if you're having

second thoughts."

Rex made himself stand away from her to give her a chance to think about what they were doing. Lauren turned to look out into the night. It was beautiful, and a little chilly. She wrapped her arms around herself, holding her elbows. When her eyes lifted to his, he knew what she was going to say.

"I think we need to cool off, just for a bit."

Actually, the same words had been going through his mind. In the heat of the moment, he'd thought that his own issues would resolve themselves, but the anxiety was still there. For his own peace of mind, they probably needed to talk about some things.

That was enough to really cool him off, and he gave her a lopsided smile. "You know, this is important enough to me to wait. You are important enough."

Lauren blinked, then tears filled her eyes. She reached out and brushed her hand against his chest. Rex felt the touch burn through the clothing, and it was difficult to remember why he'd stopped them. They both needed to think about what was happening. It was unexpected, and their actions tonight could have repercussions on the future.

With a smile, Lauren moved into his arms. She

wrapped herself around his body and rested her head on his chest. Rex wrapped his own arms around her, and they just stood there. Eventually, she drew back. "I want to thank you for a fantastic night."

Rex shook his head as he let her go. "You planned it."

"Still, you were a good sport about everything."

Rex frowned. "I had a great night. And I'll do it again whenever you're free."

She flushed and nodded, glancing away. "And thank you for slowing the train down. I have a feeling we would have had regrets tomorrow."

"Possibly," he murmured. Stepping close, he cupped her jaw in his hands and kissed her again. Had it really been that good? Oh, yeah, it had. Immediately, his body began to respond, and he had to force himself to let her go.

"You need to move on, buddy, before I change my mind," Lauren warned, followed by a grin.

Rex laughed and saluted her. "Yes, ma'am!"

He turned and got into his vehicle, but he waved her on and watched as she drove away. That woman was going to change his life.

GEN CALLED AS SOON as Lauren got in the door. Keegan and her mother had gone to a movie, and they didn't seem to be back yet, because the house was quiet. She swiped the slide on the phone. "Calling to gloat?"

"Well, I have a feeling it wasn't that good because you're home too early."

Lauren thought of what she'd almost done and smiled slightly. "Well, we decided to slow the train down."

"Oh," Gen said in a singsong voice. "So, it was good, then. You and Rex clicked?"

"Yeah, we clicked."

Gen laughed on the other end of the line.

"Go ahead and gloat," Lauren said. "Get it out of your system."

Gen laughed. "I told you! You guys are so alike in so many ways."

Lauren kicked off her shoes and headed toward the bedroom. Max lumbered into the room, and she paused to scratch behind the big shepherd's ears. Gen's mouth was running a mile a minute, so Lauren just listened.

As she listened to Gen talk about how great they would be together, Lauren felt a sense of contentment wash over her. It was nice to have someone to talk to about everything, even the mundane things. Gen was always there to listen, to offer advice or simply to commiserate. They had been friends for years, and they talked every few days. Her mother was a good person to talk to as well, but she could be more critical.

Lauren changed into her pajamas and settled into bed with her phone. Gen was still talking, but Lauren was only half-listening now. Her thoughts kept drifting back to Rex. He was so different from anyone she had ever dated before. He was smart, funny, and easy to talk to. They had spent the evening laughing and joking, and Lauren had felt completely at ease with him.

But there was something else there too, something that Lauren couldn't quite put her finger on. She had felt an attraction between them, a connection that she had never felt with anyone else. It was exciting, but also scary.

Lauren sighed and rolled onto her side. Maybe she was reading too much into things. Maybe it was just a fun evening with a cute guy. But she couldn't shake the feeling that there was more to it than that.

As she drifted off to sleep, Lauren couldn't help but wonder what the future held for her and Rex.

CHAPTER SEVEN

Rex's body was humming. Moving behind the weight bar, he positioned his hands on the bar, then planted his feet to give himself the best base. This was only one-seventy. It was a walk in the park.

Truck stood to the side, arms crossed over his heavy chest. "You done thinkin', yet?"

Rex didn't let the gibe rush him. This kind of weight was nothing to sneeze at, but Truck was not a normal lifter. Rex had seen him do two-twenty on the clean and jerks, which was creeping up toward Olympic territory. Rex didn't have that in him. Maybe if he hadn't been shot through the thigh and shoulder during the Rebellion. And if he hadn't been shot in a damn gas station weeks ago.

He shut his brain off. He didn't want to think of

that. Puffing out a breath, he jerked the weighted bar up to his chest, then, feet spreading, lifted it over his head.

Rex felt the familiar burn in his muscles as he lowered the bar back down to his chest, then pushed it up again. He repeated the movement, counting his reps silently in his head. He was focused, in the zone, and nothing else mattered. Not the past, not the future, just this moment.

Truck watched him closely, studying his form. Rex was a good lifter, but he wasn't as strong as Truck. No one was. Truck had a natural talent for lifting, and he had honed his skills over the years. Being a Delta team member, he had to be in top physical form. Rex respected him for the work he put in, even though Truck could be a bit of a jerk sometimes.

As Rex finished his set and racked the weight, Truck stepped forward. "Not bad," he said grudgingly. "But you can do better."

Rex just shrugged. He knew he could always do better, but he wasn't competing with anyone but himself. He lifted to stay in shape, to feel strong and powerful. It was a way to forget about everything, even if only for a little while. The ten-year anniversary of the Rebellion was this week, and it was bothering him more than it should have.

He wiped his forehead with the back of his hand and took a deep breath. "You ready old man?"

Truck grinned. "Sure thing, Swiss cheese." And with that, he stepped up to the bar and began to load it with weights. Rex shook his head at the new nick name Truck had come up for him. He *had* been shot a lot, but that wasn't something he could help.

Truck did his set, perfect as always, then sat next to him on the bench. "You gonna tell me what's on your mind? You don't ask for a workout unless you're stewing on something."

Rex smiled slightly, shaking his head. Truck always knew when he had something on his mind. "I met a girl."

"OH, shit," Truck crowed, laughing and smacking Rex on his shoulder. "You're in for it now, buddy. Tell me about her."

Rex hesitated. He didn't enjoy talking about himself, especially when it came to relationships. But Truck was his friend, and he trusted him. "She's...different. She's smart and funny, and she doesn't take any crap from anyone. But she's also...vulnerable, I guess you could say." He gave him a sideways look. "She's a cop. She was there when I witnessed that robbery last month, and during the mess, I kind of had a flashback."

"To Nightshade?"

Rex nodded, glancing at him. "I think the anniversary has been bugging me. I haven't had a flashback for a couple of years. Anyway, it could have gone really bad. I mean, they were about to strap me down onto a gurney."

Truck huffed, glancing at him out of the corner of his eye. "You must have been hurt pretty bad."

Rex sighed. He hadn't told Truck everything. "Bad enough. I had a through and through." He rested a hand over the injury. "But she could see things were going down in my head, and she backed everyone off. She *saw* me."

A slight smile tugged at the scar on Truck's face. "That's really something. We're very lucky if we can find someone that acknowledges our past. And isn't freaked out about it. I would be lost without my Mary."

Rex shook his head. "I haven't even told her about what happened. I mean, she knows I was in the war, but not what happened there."

Truck raised an eyebrow. "You haven't told her? You think she'll judge you for it or something?"

Rex shrugged. "I don't know. It's just...it's not

something I like to talk about. And I don't want her to see me as some kind of victim."

Truck leaned forward, his eyes serious. "Listen, Rex. You're not a victim. You're a survivor. You made it through something that most people couldn't even imagine. And if this girl is worth your time, she'll understand that. She'll respect you for it." Truck grinned at him and knocked him with his shoulder. "Sounds like you've got it bad."

Rex scowled. "I don't have it bad. I'm just... I don't know. I feel like I need to protect her, you know? From all the shit that's out there."

Truck was silent for a moment, then he leaned forward. "You're a good guy. You've been through some shit, but you've come out the other side. And if you think this girl is worth it, then go for it. Just be careful, okay?"

Rex nodded, feeling grateful for Truck's words. He knew he could always count on him to give him honest advice, even if he didn't always like it. "Thanks, man."

Rex nodded slowly, feeling a weight lift from his shoulders. Truck was right, as always. He had been through a lot, but he had come out the other side. And if this girl was as special as he thought she was, she would see that too.

"You always know how to put things in perspective."

Truck grinned. "That's what I'm here for, little man. That, and to make sure you don't drop a weight on your foot." He stood up, clapping Rex on the back. "Now come on, let's hit those squats."

* * *

Lauren frowned at the phone. "You still haven't found Chewy?"

"No," the woman on the other end said, "and we've tapped all our local CIs. He's almost eighteen now, and he knows he's going to do prison time for this."

Lauren sighed, rocking back in the chair. She'd stopped at the substation to file a couple of reports and follow up with her buddy Detective Shelly Mueller on the Quik Stop shooting. She had thought that they'd have picked him up by now.

"What about his family? Have you talked to them?" Lauren asked.

"Yes, Lauren, you know we have. I promise you, we've been keeping an eye on them. But so far, he hasn't made contact."

Lauren rubbed her temples, feeling a headache

coming on. Chewy was a low-level gang member who had been involved in a shooting a few weeks ago. He had fled the scene and had been on the run ever since. She knew he was one of literally thousands Shelly tried to keep track of on any given day.

"Thanks, Shel. Keep me updated," she said, ending the call. She leaned back in the chair, thinking. There had to be some way to find Chewy. She just had to figure out what it was.

And Rex needed to stay aware, just in case Chewy got it in his head to do something drastic. Lauren picked up her phone. They hadn't spoken for a day. After the date, he'd immediately sent her a text telling her how much he'd enjoyed himself. And she'd responded in kind. The next day she'd sent him a funny meme about nurses, and he'd sent her a laugh emoji. That had been two days ago.

Lauren took a deep breath and dialed Rex's number. As the phone rang, she tried to push aside her concerns about Chewy and focus on her personal life for a moment.

"Hey, Lauren," Rex answered on the third ring. "What's up?"

"Not much, just checking in," Lauren replied, trying to sound casual. "How are you doing?"

"I'm good," Rex said. "Just got off shift a little while ago and I'm heading to the gym. You?"

"I'm at the station, working on tracking down a suspect," Lauren said. "It's been a bit of a headache."

"Sorry to hear that," Rex said sympathetically. "Is there anything I can do to help?"

Lauren smiled to herself, feeling grateful for his support. "Actually, there is. I just want you to be aware of your surroundings. I talked to the detective on the case, and they still can't find Chew. I was thinking maybe you could keep an eye out for him. He's the suspect I'm trying to find, and I'm worried he might do something stupid."

"Of course," Rex said without hesitation. "I'll keep an eye out for him, and I'll let you know if I see anything. I seriously doubt he'd come after me."

"Well, he has prison time hanging over his head, so I would rather you be safe than sorry."

"No problem," Rex said. "I appreciate your concern. So, uh, do you want to get together again soon?"

Lauren felt a flutter of excitement in her stomach. "Yeah, I'd like that," she said, trying not to sound too eager. "How about breakfast tomorrow morning?"

"Sounds great," Rex said. "I'll text you later with a few options."

Lauren smiled, feeling grateful for the distraction from work. "Looking forward to it," she said. "See you then."

"See you," Rex said, and they hung up.

Lauren felt a surge of energy as she hung up. For a moment, she just sat and enjoyed the sensation. It wasn't very often that a guy made her tummy flutter, but Rex definitely did. She glanced around the substation. There were a few other cops doing reports at their own cubicles, and a couple were giving pass-on information to the next shift. Several of the guys she worked with were handsome and available, but they were like her brothers.

Lauren shook her head, trying to clear her thoughts. She had a job to do, and she couldn't let her personal life distract her from that. She took a deep breath and focused on the task at hand. Chew was still out there, and she needed to find him before he hurt anyone else.

Lauren logged back into the computer and continued searching for leads on Chew's where-abouts. She pulled up his criminal record, looking for any connections or patterns that might lead her to him. As she dug deeper, she realized that Chew had a history of violence and drug abuse. He had been in and out of juvie several times, and it was clear that he was not going to change his ways soon.

Lauren knew that Chew was a dangerous young man, and she needed to be careful. She took a moment to text Rex Chew's most up-to-date picture, reminding him to be cautious and to let her know if he saw anything suspicious. Rex replied quickly, assuring her he would keep an eye out and that he was looking forward to seeing her tomorrow.

Lauren smiled, glancing around the room. No one was paying attention to her, and she was very glad. If they saw her all moon-eyed, she'd be teased unmercifully. That was how being a cop was. You got teased and harassed constantly, but when the shit hit the fan, there was a wall of blue behind you to support you. She loved being a cop.

A few minutes later, Diego dropped a hand on her shoulder. "You're not going to find this kid tonight. You need to head home and get some rest."

Lauren knew he was right, so she logged out and packed up her gear. "You're right, I know."

"You okay?" Diego asked, stopping to look her in the eye. "You're taking this one kind of personal."

"Well," Lauren said, then she hesitated. Diego was her partner, though, and he needed to know.

"Remember the guy from the Quik Stop that rendered aid? Kind of got injured himself?"

"Yeah, the vet."

"Right," she glanced around to make sure they weren't being overheard. "I was set up on a blind date with him through a mutual friend. And I really like him."

Diego's dark eyes went soft, and one side of his mouth kicked up. "No way," he breathed. "You're dating? Good for you, Lauren."

Lauren felt the blood rush to her cheeks. Diego was her best friend in the department, and she looked up to him as a father figure. She'd been to his house for family dinners. She'd watched two of his girls graduate. It meant a lot to her that he was okay with this. "I won't let it negatively affect my job. I am determined to find Chewy, though."

Diego nodded, parking his hands on his gun belt. "Of course, you are. I understand a little better now. Tonight, when we come in, we'll knock on a few doors. See if we can spook a response." He grinned at her and winked, and she laughed.

"Sounds like a plan."

He turned and left the squad room. She knew he would head to the gym before he went home.

Lauren grabbed her gear bag and followed him

out. On the drive home, she replayed in her mind all the conversations she and Rex had had. And she tried to understand why he excited her the way he did.

Her phone rang as she was pulling in the drive. She parked and looked down at the screen. Rex.

"Hey, what's going on?"

There was silence on the other end of the line, and she grew concerned. "Rex?"

"Yeah, I'm here," he said, his voice more gruff than normal.

Lauren frowned, not liking the emotion she heard in those three words. "Are you okay, Rex?"

"Yeah," he sighed. "I didn't even realize I was calling you until I heard your voice. I'm sorry, I know you must be home with your son now."

Lauren glanced at the watch on her wrist. Keegan would get up in about half an hour. The sun wasn't even up yet. "Nah, it's early, yet. He's still in bed."

"Oh," he said.

Lauren waited for more, but he was silent for several long seconds. "What's wrong, Rex?"

She heard him swallow on the other end of the line, and she knew he was upset, but she gave him time to get the words out.

"I don't know," Rex finally admitted. "I guess I'm

just feeling overwhelmed. It's been a tough few weeks at work, and...I don't know. I feel like I'm stuck in a rut, you know? Like I'm just going through the motions."

Lauren felt a pang of sympathy for him. She had felt that way before, too. "I understand," she said softly. "It's hard when you feel like you're not making progress or you're not seeing results."

"Yeah," he agreed. "And then there's... other stuff."

"Other stuff?" Lauren prompted gently.

Rex hesitated for a moment before speaking. "Just... memories," he said finally. "Things I try not to think about, but they keep creeping back in."

Lauren's heart went out to him. She knew Rex had served in the military, and he had mentioned before that he had seen some rough stuff during his time overseas. "I'm sorry," she said. "That sounds really tough."

"Yeah," he said again. "I'm sorry for dumping all of this on you. It was a hard night, and it's the anniversary of a really bad day, and I think it's all just weighing on me."

"I understand. Do you want to tell me about your night?"

Rex took a deep breath. "Had a wild patient. Former Marine. He survived a botched suicide attempt, but his brain was deprived of oxygen for a long time, and he's going to have long-lasting repercussions. His fine motor-skills were damaged and he's going to be in a wheelchair for a while. Anyway, he wakes up out of a medically induced coma tonight and he realizes what has happened, and the look on his face…" Rex paused, and she heard him swallow again. "It was utter despair. He started crying and begging us to let him die. We had to sedate him to get him to calm down."

Lauren's eyes filled with tears, and she had to blink them away to see the steering wheel. "That has to be so hard," she said softly.

Rex choked out a laugh. "You have no idea. I'm going to tell you something I've never told another living soul, Lauren. I've wanted to do the same thing. Just end it all."

"No," Lauren cried immediately, sitting up in the seat. The thought of big, vibrant Rex reaching that point was abhorrent to her, and all of her training went out the window. "Suicide is never the answer. Never. I'm sorry for your patient and that you had to care for him, but you don't say that, Rex. Please." She forced the tears back, and took a calming breath, and she dredged up her training. "I hear you, and I hear the pain in your voice. I'm sorry you've felt so alone. But you're not alone."

"I know," Rex said finally. "And I know I have support. I have a couple of really good nurse friends I call when it gets bad. I tried to call Olivia tonight, but her phone is going to voicemail. Baylee isn't answering either. They were friends I served with on Nightshade."

Lauren's blood chilled at the name Nightshade. Oh, that clarified a lot of things. The ten-year anniversary of the 'Rebellion' was this week, and it had been all over the news. No wonder he was walking that line, if he had been there. It was recorded as one of the worst attacks on military personnel in history, and her heart ached for him. She had a feeling he had seen incredible atrocities, and it was no wonder his heart hurt.

"Rex, why don't you come over and have breakfast with us?"

Lauren didn't know who was more surprised, her or Rex. She hadn't even planned to say it. It had just popped into her mouth. Or out of, she supposed. But it felt right. Her mother wouldn't mind. Actually, her mother would be thrilled that she was inviting a man over. Hopefully, she would disappear into her little space, though, and leave them alone.

Rex needed a connection right now, and she didn't mind being that for him.

"I don't know," he said, sounding a little clearer. "I didn't call you to feel sorry for me," he said, voice gruff.

"I don't feel sorry for you," she told him truthfully. "But you need someone right now, and I'm willing to be that someone."

There was a long silence, then he cleared his throat. "Are you sure?"

"Positive," she said firmly. "Come over and have breakfast. We have a spare room, so you can crash while I get some sleep. And when we get up, we can talk more. If you want. No pressure. Maybe just stop and get some orange juice on the way. Plus, we have all the free fur therapy you need."

CHAPTER EIGHT

So, that's what he did. An hour later, Rex was pulling into her driveway and getting out of the truck, juice bottle in hand.

As he walked up to her front door, Rex couldn't help feeling a mix of emotions. Gratitude, for Lauren's kindness and willingness to help him. But also a sense of vulnerability, as he was about to enter a stranger's home and share his struggles with someone he'd only just met.

Lauren greeted him warmly at the door, a smile on her face that put him at ease. "Hey, come on in," she said, leading him to the kitchen, where the smell of pancakes and bacon filled the air.

"Wow, this looks amazing," Rex said, looking

around at the spread of food on the table. "You didn't have to go to all this trouble."

"Nonsense," Lauren said, pouring him a cup of coffee. "It's no trouble at all. I love cooking, and I love having people over. It's one of the ways I show love. This is my mom, Sophia."

Rex leaned around and shook the older woman's hand, noting the resemblance between mother and daughter.

"Pleasure to meet you, Rex," Sophia said, taking the juice from him.

A boy with messy, dirty-blond hair entered the room, a sleepy smile on his face. Rex thought Lauren had said he was twelve, but he seemed kind of small to be a preteen. Rex held out his hand. "Keegan, right? Your mom talks about you a lot."

The boy rolled his brown eyes. "Of course, she does." But he shook Rex's hand like a man. Then he turned to the table. "Where's the bacon?"

"Sit down and eat," Lauren told the boy. "Grandma's going to drive you in today."

The two women shared a look, and Rex wondered how much he was disrupting their schedule. Keegan took a seat at the table, and Lauren motioned to the one beside Keegan. Then the two women sat to the left.

They began passing plates of food around. Rex didn't really think he was hungry, but he changed his mind as the scent of bacon hit him hard. That was when he realized he hadn't eaten for hours. The last thing he'd gotten had been a yogurt out of one of the machines. And he'd eaten it on the run.

"This looks amazing," he said, taking some bacon.

"Well, we made plenty," Lauren's mom said, smiling at him.

Sophia looked just like her daughter, with long blondish hair with streaks of gray, and striking blue eyes. A perpetual smile curved her lips, like the world itself amused her. He could tell by the lines around her eyes that she'd seen a lot in the world, but there was an obvious strength to her.

Which had carried over to her daughter. Rex looked at Lauren. She'd changed out of her uniform. She now wore a well-worn gray t-shirt with SAPD over her luscious breasts, and blue jeans. Her hair hung down her back in a casual braid, and Rex wanted to reach over and let the braid slide through his fingers. That would probably freak her out. He was kind of fascinated by the length of it. In a bun there was no way to know how long it had been.

Memories of their kiss haunted him, and he

wondered if she'd thought about it as much as he had.

He glanced around the kitchen. This was the heart of their home. It was a well-used area, a little cluttered but not dirty. It reminded him of his grandmother's house, who he hadn't thought of for many years. She'd been gone a long time, but he remembered her kitchen as being warm and inviting, and she always had candy or sweets for the kids.

Rex ate two plates of food, enough that Keegan gave him wide eyes. "Hey," he said defensively, "I'm a growing boy."

Keegan snickered before picking up his empty plate to take to the sink.

"Backpack," Lauren asked.

Keegan nodded. "Got it. And the permission slip."

"Excellent," she said, walking him to the door. She pressed a kiss to the top of his head. "I'll see you this afternoon, buddy."

"Bye, Mom," the boy called as he jogged down the steps. "Bye, Rex. Nice to meet you."

"Nice to meet you too, buddy," Rex said, surprised at the acknowledgement.

Lauren closed the door behind her mother and turned to him with a smile. "That kid is my heart."

"I can understand why," Rex said, nodding as he sat back in the chair. "He seems like a great kid. I can tell you've raised him right."

Lauren's smile deepened, and she gave him a nod. "Thank you. It hasn't been easy being a single parent.

"I can only imagine," Rex said. "But you've done a great job."

Lauren shrugged. "I've just done what I had to do. Keegan is the priority."

"That's what being a parent is all about."

Lauren gathered the dirty dishes, placing them in the dishwasher. Rex stood and began helping her. "Thank you again for breakfast. It was incredible. My stomach is so tight."

Lauren glanced at him sideways. "You can probably stand to gain a few pounds."

Rex grimaced. "I'm supposed to be at the gym right now, but this was more appealing today."

Lauren sent him a smile. "Well, let me get these loaded and you can come out with me to feed. I'll give you a workout."

Rex blinked. "Feed?"

Lauren grinned at him. "You're not going to just loaf around. I'm going to put your ass to work. Then you're going to sleep for a while, and it will be some of the best sleep you've had because I worked you."

Rex laughed. "I already worked my shift."

"Well, I did too. But the animals need care, and I can't go to sleep until they're taken care of."

Ten minutes later, they were walking outside. It was a beautiful Texas morning, with a steady breeze blowing in from the west and a brilliant blue sky overhead. Rex took a minute to glance over the property. He hadn't really noticed it when he'd arrived. "You have a beautiful place, here."

The house was in the center of the property, and there were pastures out front and behind. There was a large red barn to the right of the house, and when they started in that direction, several voices raised to greet them. Three dogs came out from the barn. One was definitely a German Shepherd, but the other two seemed like mixed-breeds, weighing in about eighty pounds each.

"This is Max, Willow and Minnie. They wander the acreage, keeping predators away."

"Hi, guys," Rex said, reaching out to greet the animals. They all three crowded around his legs, eager for attention. He smiled, sinking his fingers into thick fur. "Good dogs…"

Lauren led him into the barn. There was a chorus of cries from the left.

"This is Burner," she said, motioning to a large, dark horse who pushed to the front of the group. "Ranger and Mistress. We call her Missy. They're all good horses, but pigs."

Rex laughed as they stood in line for treats Lauren pulled from her pocket. Then she slipped inside with the huge animals and opened a pipe gate. They bolted out of the barn, Burner in the lead. They ran around the enclosure, bucking and playing and making fools of themselves. Rex laughed as he watched them. Lauren was grinning as she left the stall. "They're idiots," she said, but he could hear the love in her voice.

Lauren turned and moved down the barn, stopping at another stall. "These are our alpacas. The dark one is Remy, our male, and the white one is Lola, the female. They're a little more shy, but they'll warm up to you, eventually."

Rex looked at the oddly shaped animals and shook his head. He'd seen alpacas before, but never this close. A goat jumped up on the inside of the stall, obviously wanting treats. He bleated pathetically, and Lauren handed Rex a treat. "That's Ponch.

Jon is in the corner over there. They're little bastards and will be in your face every chance they get."

Rex laughed and handed the goat the biscuit. "Ponch and Jon? From Chips?"

Lauren grinned and nodded. "I'm surprised you recognize the names!"

"It was one of my favorite shows when I was a kid," he said, grinning. "All reruns, of course, but I didn't care. I wanted a motorcycle so bad. I drove my mom nuts, begging for one."

"It was one of my favorites, too, for entirely different reasons." Lauren gave him a bawdy wink, and Rex laughed.

He hadn't known what to expect coming out here today, and truth be told, he was a little ashamed of needing her. They had had one single date, and he was already calling her for a rescue. He realized, though, that he'd needed this distraction more than anything. "Thank you," he said, leaning against the stall to look her in the eye. "I haven't laughed for a while, and I think I needed it."

Lauren leaned against the stall boards as well and gave him a lop-sided smile. "We all need some kind of release from the tension. I'm glad you found some peace out here."

Rex glanced around. "This is not my normal

environment. I wasn't a city boy, per se, but I'm definitely more familiar with urban settings."

She shrugged. "Maybe. People are adaptable, though. And sometimes you need to be shaken out of your rut. I think you've fallen into the problem a lot of carers do: you care for everyone else to the exclusion of yourself. And that wears on you. Like the guy you dealt with today. You empathized with him to the point that you lost your objectivity."

Rex blinked and frowned. "You're right. I totally lost my objectivity."

Lauren moved across the way and unstacked two bales of hay. "Park it," she said, motioning to one.

"Yes, Officer," Rex said, smiling. Damn, she was bossy. But they settled on the bales, with their backs against the opposite stalls.

"I didn't realize you'd been in the Rebellion."

Rex sighed, glancing at her from the corner of his eye. "It's not something I like to tell people. Plus, it's been ten years. Most people have forgotten it."

"Mm, I don't think people have forgotten it," she corrected. "Especially not right now, with all the commemorative stuff going on."

"Yeah," Rex murmured. "I hate all the commemorative stuff. The balloons and parades and now it's a national holiday. So, every year I'm going to have to 'show thankfulness to our military'. It's a crock of shit."

"Why do you say that?" she asked gently.

Rex struggled with what to tell her. "It was the hardest day of my life. They have no idea what I went through, and if they haven't been in the military, I doubt they'll ever understand."

"I would like to understand," she said softly, reaching out to rest her hand on his wrist. "I work with a lot of vets, but I'm sure your story is different."

Rex almost jerked back from her touch, but he forced himself to stay still as he looked into her eyes. They were calm and steady, just as she was, and he kind of wanted to tell her what had happened that day. None of his former girlfriends had known. Hell, none of them had asked. They preferred to be oblivious to the source of his pain. They ignored the late-night rambling and the mood swings. Rex knew he was a little fucked up in the head, but Lauren made him feel like he could handle it.

For three years he'd gone to therapy, but it seemed like they just wanted to push pills at him to get him to forget. That didn't seem to be healthy, so he'd politely backed away. The flashbacks had receded, so he hadn't felt like he'd needed the in-depth care anymore.

"Nightshade was this small forward operating base in the middle of nowhere," he sighed. "The Taliban were ramping up the attacks, and we were dealing with a lot of wounded. We had gone almost twenty-four hours without sleep, some of us. Because they kept bringing us wounded. You can't sleep if you know you have guys bleeding out, so we kept going." He shrugged, turning to stare off into the distance. "They breached the walls and killed most of the Marines on the base. They came in and slaughtered all the men we'd just worked on, injured soldiers on gurneys, all of them." He made a motion with his hand. "Then they pushed the bodies into piles. It was horrific. They left us alive, because we were obviously medical and posed no threat. The soldiers that survived... the Taliban tortured. Then they would give them to us to fix up as best we could before they tortured them again. No one lasted. They killed most of them. And when we tried to fight, they shot us."

His hand went to his thigh instinctively. "I tried to stand up to them and they got me in the thigh and the shoulder. My friends Olivia and Baylee patched me up." His voice drifted off as he remembered being on that gurney, and feeling the forceps scrape the bone as Olivia pulled out the bullet. An echo of pain rolled through his body. He could deal with the pain, though. The girls had worse issues to deal with. Olivia had lost a leg that day, and Baylee... well.

Lauren's hand slipped down to his own, and she held it tight. Rex tried not to squeeze too tightly in response. There was more to tell, but he didn't think he was ready yet.

"Anyway," he shook his head. "It was bad. I'm not going to weigh you down with it."

Lauren seemed to sense that he just didn't want to talk about it anymore, so she gave him a nod. "Okay, then. Well, just know that I'm here if you change your mind."

Rex gave her a lopsided grin and leaned forward to drop a light kiss to her mouth. She tasted of laughter and sweetness, and he wanted to just bask in her.

Before he could pull away, Lauren cupped his face in her hands. That was all the encouragement he needed. Rex deepened the kiss, burrowing his fingers into her hair at the nape of her neck. Lauren's mouth softened and opened, and Rex lost himself in the feel of her. And the taste of her. God, she was so sweet.

When they drew apart, they were both breathing a little heavy. Her expression seemed a little shocked, and he had a feeling his did as well. Where the hell had that come from?

"I didn't expect that," Lauren said softly. She blinked and sat back on the bale. "But I should have after the other night."

"I didn't either," Rex admitted. Then, unable to help himself, he leaned forward to kiss her again.

Grinning, Lauren turned her face up to meet him, and he thought she was as anxious as he was to see if it had been a fluke.

It was no fluke.

When they drew apart, they were panting, and Rex was shook. He'd never... wow.

Lauren had a bit of a poker face, but he could tell she'd been affected as well. There was a flush to her fair skin, and her eyes were bright. She was simply beautiful.

"Well," she said brusquely, "we need to get moving. We have work to do before we can head into the house."

"Okay," he said, brushing his hands on his jeans. "Tell me what you need me to do."

Twenty minutes later, Rex found himself in a horse stall with an oddly shaped rake in his hands.

He was supposed to pick up the horse turds and put them in the wheelbarrow, leaving the good, clean bedding behind. It was basic work, but within a few minutes his t-shirt was molded to his chest with sweat. No, he wasn't lifting, but this would do for exercise today.

He glanced out the door in time to see Lauren pass by, a huge sack of something over her shoulder. "Lauren, let me get that," he said quickly, setting the rake to the side.

Lauren didn't pause, though, just continued on to what she'd called the tack room. It was where all the food and equipment was stored. She shrugged the weight off her shoulder and to the edge of the bin, then she pulled on a string and the top completely opened up. She dumped the bag into the can, then folded the empty bag.

"I do it all the time," she said, smiling.

Rex was impressed. He'd only been out here a little while, and it was obvious how much work there was. "You do this every morning after work?"

She nodded, using a large aluminum scoop to portion grain out into buckets. "I do. Unless I'm really backed up or working overtime, then Mom will cover. They're mostly my responsibility. Not that I mind, though. I live for this part of my day."

He could see that. She loved these animals, and they loved her in return. Rex had thought about getting a dog when he moved down here, but he couldn't guarantee his hours, and a dog needed more care than what he could give it.

He looked down. One of the big pups had kind of adopted him. Everywhere he went, the dog followed him. He thought it was Minnie, but he wasn't positive.

"Did you get the stall mucked?"

He nodded. "I need to pull the wheelbarrow out."

He went to go do that, feeling good about what he'd done for her. Maybe he'd shortened her workload a bit.

When he returned, she was doling out the feed to the animals. They crowded around her, bleating and crying. The three horses in the next pasture paced along the dividing fence, waiting for theirs. Lauren fed everyone, then came out to lean against the fence beside him.

"This was not how I expected my morning to go," he admitted.

She glanced at him, squinting in the sun. "How do you normally deal with traumatic nights?"

He sighed, looking out at the animals. "I go work out, sometimes for a really long time. I call a buddy to go with me sometimes. He was one of the Delta Force operators that helped rescue us, so he understands. Then I would head home and try to crash. Sleep is hard sometimes, though."

"My ex would bolt up out of bed, fully aware and usually reaching for a gun. Or he would drink himself into oblivion and sleep most of the next day away. It changed depending upon the stress he thought he was under."

"Yeah, I get that. I don't let myself drink like that. It would be too easy to get into trouble."

"Yes," she sighed, and he wondered what she'd had to deal with her ex. He hoped Keegan hadn't had a lot of interaction with his father like that. It would warp a kid.

"Let's go in," she murmured. "The night is starting to catch up with me."

Rex pulled in a deep breath of fresh air. "You know, I think it is me, too. Thank you, Lauren, for inviting me out."

"Of course," she said, smiling broadly.

Lauren led him into the house, then back through a hallway to the last door on the left. "This is the spare room. There's a Jack and Jill bathroom through there. You can wash up or shower up, whatever you need to do. Mom will be home in a bit, but she'll be quiet, so sleep as long as you want. Pull the blackout curtains."

"Okay." He looked at her for a long moment, wondering if he dared try for another kiss. What the hell. Leaning in, he captured her mouth. It was supposed to be no more than a peck, but something changed. Intensified. Cupping her head in his hand, he deepened the kiss. Lauren was a complex mix of strength and vulnerability, and he wanted to learn every aspect of her, because what he'd seen so far only intrigued him more.

When she sighed and stepped into his space, her body flush against his, he almost jerked away. The feeling of her so close, so very warm, was enough to send his heart rate galloping.

But then she kissed him back with the same fervor, and he knew he couldn't stop now even if he tried. He deepened the kiss, his hands roaming over her body. She gasped when he cupped her plump breast, her nipple already hard under his touch. He broke the kiss, leaning back to look at her. Her face was flushed, her lips swollen from his kisses.

"I swear to you, this isn't why I came here. Are you sure you want to do this?" he asked, his voice rough with emotion.

"More than anything," she replied, pulling him back in for another kiss.

Rex kissed her for a moment, then broke away to pick her up, carrying her to the bed. Gently laying her down, he hovered over her, his eyes locked with hers. She reached up, pulling his face down to hers for another kiss. Slowly, he began to undress her, his hands reverently tracing the shape of her body.

Lauren was a strong woman, but she had curves in all the right places. Rex wanted to wander, but there was a building need that he couldn't deny. Judging by her enthusiasm, she was in the same boat. "How long will your mother be gone?"

"Hours," Lauren whispered. "She has a book club meeting at the library."

That was all the encouragement he needed. He looked down. Everything was gone except her panties and her bra, and as much as he wanted to draw out the anticipation, he needed to see her, and those breasts he'd been dreaming of. He reached behind her back, and she arched up for him. One-handed, he managed to unfasten her bra. She pulled it away with no modesty, and he had to admit, she had nothing to be shy about. Her breasts were perfection. Full and round, with dark pink nipples. Rex leaned down and pulled one nipple into his mouth, using the tip of his tongue to swirl around it.

Lauren gasped, clutching at his head, and her hips arched up. "That feels wonderful," she moaned.

Rex shifted to the other nipple. And it was as sweet as the first. He could make a feast of her breasts. He knew there were other places on her body he was going to love too, though.

Drawing back, he knelt at the end of the bed and slowly drew her panties down her long legs. Oh, she was perfection. From the low-lidded, languorous look in her eyes to the delicate pink polish on her toes, she was all woman. Her hips flared out, and he could envision gripping them in his hands as he was pounding into her.

Lauren must have grown impatient, because one of her legs cocked out, and he recognized the welcome when he saw it. Rex stepped off the bed and shucked his clothes, pausing for a moment to go to his bag. There was a rubber in his Dopp kit, and he ripped it open as he walked back to the bed. Lauren's eyes had gone wide as she watched him, and Rex felt a wave of satisfaction.

He went to the gym for several reasons, but right then, he couldn't remember one. He was just glad he did, for the look of appreciation in her eyes.

Rolling the condom down his erection, he knew Lauren watched him. So, he took an extra few seconds as he moved toward her, fist wrapped around his dick.

"You're teasing me," she murmured.

"Am I?" he grinned.

"If you knew how wet I was…" she turned her head, her eyes closing as she clenched her legs together.

Rex lay down beside her, his right hand going down to tickle at the patch of hair between her legs. "Let me see," he murmured, sliding his middle finger down.

Oh, yeah, she was wet and hot. His dick throbbed. "Damn, girl," he murmured, nudging her thighs open with his hand. It was very easy to find her swollen clit. Rex stroked his finger up and down, rubbing against the little bundle of nerves, and Lauren drew in a shaky breath.

"Yes," she sighed, "right there."

Rex wanted her to come at least once before he joined her, because once he buried himself in her sweetness, he had a feeling there would be no holding back. So, he rubbed her with his finger, following her body as she shifted her hips, tilting up into his touch. Leaning over, he tongued her nipple at the same time. He thought it would take a few minutes, but within just a few seconds, she was arching beneath his touch and crying out. Her thighs closed on his hand, but he continued to circle his finger, gently drawing her orgasm out.

For the first time in a long time, he realized that her pleasure was more important than his own. If she pushed him away right now and said they were done, he would be disappointed, but okay with it. He'd been with women before when the emotional connection had been lacking, and the difference was obvious. The sight of her release satisfied him almost as much as his own orgasm.

When she reached around him, though, and tugged him up, he went. Her body cradled him, and he could feel the heat from her core. He looked down into her languid eyes, and he knew he was falling hard and fast, but he couldn't do anything about it.

LAUREN WAS STILL QUAKING from her release, but she knew she wanted more. Rex came to her, nestling his hardness between her thighs. If she shifted the tiniest bit, she could pull him inside. She was desperate to feel him inside her.

When she looked up into his face, though, she paused. There was a look in his eyes... "Are you okay?"

He grinned at her, a flash of straight white teeth. "I am. I'm just relishing this."

Lauren grinned as well, her hands running over his broad shoulders and down his arms. Then she circled in, wandering over his pecs and abs. She teased his dark chest hair for a moment, before moving downward. Rex's eyes blinked shut as she wrapped her hand around his length, running her thumb over the crown of his penis. Even through the condom, she could feel how hard and needy he was. There was moisture inside the tip of the condom.

"Well, just so you know, this isn't a one and done," she whispered, nibbling at his jaw. "We might do this a couple of times."

He gave her a shake of his head, his mouth twisting. "Nope, only one condom."

Oh. Damn. She knew she didn't have any. Fuck. "Well, we'd better make sure this is good, then, hm?"

Rex bared his teeth at her in a cocky smile. "I don't think we have to worry about that."

Lauren glided her other hand down his side to his hip. When he'd grabbed the condom, she'd seen the scars on his hips, and she felt them now, but she didn't say anything about them. If he wanted to tell her what they were from, he could, but she wasn't going to push.

Besides, nothing was allowed to bring them down now.

Shifting her hips and tilting up, she pulled just the head of him inside her.

"Oh, damn you, I was trying to take it slow," he growled, kissing down from her ear.

Lauren chuckled, then gasped as he pushed a little deeper. "Oh," she murmured, her eyes falling closed. She turned her head, needing to taste him again. He must have had the same thought, because they met in the middle. As his tongue glided against hers, he flexed his hips, then retracted. Lauren thought she was ready for the feel of him, but it had been a while. All the prep work in the world wouldn't help her accommodate his size, so she had to deliberately un-tense her body. Even then, it took a few moments for her body to take him.

Then he was seated as deeply as he could go, and Lauren moved her head so she could breathe out. Damn, he felt good...

They began to move together, and it was as if they'd been lovers for years. Rex moved exactly as she liked, and within less than a minute, she was on the edge of joy again. He seemed to sense how close she was, because he drew to a stop, panting in her ear. They were both on the edge, she realized. His back and arms quaked as he tried not to move.

Unable to hold still, she began nibbling kisses along his jaw. He turned his head and took her mouth, kissing her one way and then another, then delving deeper. Lauren rocked her hips, and they were off again. This time, though, she could tell by the way he arched that there would be no stopping. He powered into her, and it was exactly what she wanted.

The orgasm that hit her this time was epic, and she cried out, clutching at his ass cheeks as she pulled him into her. She didn't want him to stop moving, and she didn't want the pleasure to end.

Rex groaned and went still above her, and Lauren could feel his body tip over the edge of orgasm. He surged into her once, twice, three more times, so hard, before he groaned long and loud, and collapsed against her.

Lauren quivered beneath him, holding him as tightly as she could. Eventually, he propped himself on his elbows, but he kept his face turned into her neck, pressing gentle kisses there. When he lifted it, he kissed her, his body moving slightly within her. "I don't want to pull out," he whispered.

Lauren grinned, even as she kissed him. "I don't want you to pull out either. That was... something."

"I didn't go too hard, did I? There at the end, I kind of lost myself."

She shook her head slightly. "No, it was perfect."

They slept then, and it was nice to have a warm body to curl up against. After a couple of hours, though, Lauren got antsy. If her mother came home now, there would be a lot of explaining to do. "I'm going to go to my room," she murmured.

Rex grinned. "Is Sophia going to be upset with me?"

Lauren shook her head, laughing, as she slipped out of the bed. "No, but she's going to ask me what I'm thinking. So, I'd better get some sleep before then."

Rex was staring at her body, and Lauren cocked a hip for him. No, she didn't work out as much as he did, but she had a good body that worked for her.

"I love looking at you," he told her, rolling onto his side. "Your breasts are amazing."

Her eyes flicked down the cobbles of his stomach. "You're not too hard on the eyes, either," she laughed. Leaning down, she pressed a lingering kiss to his mouth. "Get some sleep, Rex Neptune."

Then she turned and walked out, feeling his gaze on her body the entire way before she closed the door softly behind her.

CHAPTER NINE

Lauren tossed and turned for a while, replaying the night in her head. Rex was physically imposing, but he'd kissed her so gently. And he'd loved her so thoroughly. When people found out she was a cop, men specifically, they seemed to need to dominate her. She didn't feel anything like that with Rex. He was gentle and soft-spoken, and she wondered what he would look like when he was angry. Because she'd seen that with her ex. Normally, Sam was a laid-back guy, but when the devils were after him, he changed into someone completely different. She had feared for her life and her son's life more than once, and it was what had eventually driven her away. Just to be sure, she'd recorded a couple of incidents to guarantee he would not get custody of their son.

She couldn't see Rex doing the same thing. He had better self-control, and he'd been dealing with his own stress longer than Sam had when they'd split up.

She definitely didn't want Keegan in the same situation they'd been in before.

Before she jumped into anything, she would be as sure as she could be about him.

Once she drifted off to sleep, she slept well, and woke feeling refreshed and happy. She showered and cleaned up, and when she headed downstairs, her mother was sitting at the kitchen table, nursing a cup of coffee as she read a book.

"Hey, Mom."

"Hello, darling. You look refreshed."

Lauren grinned. "Well, that's better than 'you look like crap, Lauren.'"

Her mother snorted. "I was trying to give you some constructive criticism."

"Hm," Lauren murmured, heading toward the coffeepot. She poured a cup, then moved to sit across from her mother, glancing out the drive to see if his car was still there. "No sign of our guest?"

Mom shook her head. "Not a sound, either."

Lauren's brows popped up. "Really? Maybe he's sleeping well, then."

Maybe she'd fucked him into unconsciousness, she thought, smirking to herself.

When she glanced up, her mother was watching her. Lauren flushed. "What?"

Sophia shook her head. "Nothing, I suppose. Just be careful, Lauren."

Lauren nodded once. "You know I always am."

Her mother gave her that arch look again, but Lauren had reached the limit for her criticism. Pushing up from the table, she dumped the coffee in the sink. "I'm going to the barn."

She needed to burn off some energy.

Keegan got home from school a few minutes later, playing with the dogs as he walked up the driveway. "Is that guy still here?"

Lauren smiled. "Yes, he is. He's still sleeping, so if you would be quiet, I would appreciate it."

Her son gave her a narrow-eyed look. "Do you like him?"

Lauren sat on the top step of the porch. "I do, actually. I think he's a decent guy."

Keegan shifted his bulging backpack and Lauren reached out to the wood beside her, patting it. Keegan sank down, sighing as he dropped his pack.

"Looks like you have a of homework."

"Yeah, I do. Mrs. Enos is just rude. She gave us two chapters of history to go over tonight."

Lauren winced. "That is no fun. How about I cover your chores tonight?"

He shrugged, rubbing Max's ear. "It just takes a second to feed the dogs. You can take the trash out, though," he grinned at her, and Lauren had to laugh.

She rolled her eyes for affect. "I guess," she sighed, but she wrapped her arm around her son's shoulders. He was growing so fast…

"I have a feeling Grandma has a snack for you. Why don't you go get it and get started on your history?"

"Yeah, I better, I guess. Love you, Mom."

"Love you too, buddy. Maybe this weekend we can go do something."

His dark eyes lightened with interest. "Like what?"

She shrugged. "I don't know. It'd been a while since we've been on a ride. Or maybe just a hike? I'll let you pick."

He cocked his head and pursed his lips. "I'll think about it."

Then he darted into the house, the dog on his heels.

It was almost an hour later when Rex came out of the bedroom and wandered into the kitchen. He was very sleep-rumpled and cute in his t-shirt and sweats shorts, and Lauren had to turn away to hide her smile. She finished washing up the few dishes in the sink, setting them in the drainer. Her mother was taking a nap in her recliner in her room, with a book spread across her chest, probably. If she had seen Rex, she surely would have remarked upon how cute he was.

Lauren turned around and smiled. "Would you like a glass of iced tea?"

"Please," Rex said. "I'm parched. I think that's the longest I've slept in a long time."

Lauren poured them each a glass of tea, handing his across the table. He took it and drank half down, leaning back in the chair. "How long have you been up?"

She shrugged lightly. "About an hour. I like to get up before Keegan gets home."

"I didn't even hear him come in."

"He's used to Mom working odd shifts and creeping around the house."

Rex nodded, taking another sip of his tea. "Your son seems like a good guy."

Lauren smiled, feeling a warmth spread through her chest. "He is. I'm lucky to have him."

They sat in comfortable silence for a few moments, the only sounds coming from the hum of the refrigerator and the distant sound of a car driving by. Rex looked up at her, his eyes soft and curious.

"Can I ask you something?"

Lauren's heart skipped a beat. "Sure."

He took a deep breath. "What happened between us this morning…was that just a one-time thing?"

Lauren felt her cheeks flush with heat. She had been wondering the same thing but hadn't known how to bring it up. "I don't know," she said honestly. "I guess it depends on what you want."

Rex leaned forward, eyes intense as he rested his elbows on the table. "I want you, Lauren. I've been wanting you for a while, now, before we were even set up. I dreamed about you, you know."

"What?" she said, feeling a little faint, which was so out of character.

He nodded, sitting back with his glass. "I did. I dreamed of being shot in that convenience store repeatedly, but you were always there to help me out. You were always there to pull me out of the flashback."

She blinked, not sure what to make of that. "I'm glad… thinking of me helped you. But why did you dream of being shot?" she asked, her voice barely above a whisper.

Rex shrugged, his expression turning serious. "I was in the military, Lauren. I saw some things that I can never forget. I've been trying to deal with my PTSD for years now. Sometimes it's better, sometimes it's worse. I've gone to counseling over the years. Sometimes it helps, sometimes it doesn't. Before the robbery, I had gone without flashbacks for several years. But being pinned down and shot dredged it all back up."

Lauren's heart ached for him. She could see the pain and the wariness in his eyes. "I'm sorry you had to go through that. But I'm here for you. And I think… I think I want to be with you, too."

Rex smiled, a slow grin spreading across his face. "Good. Because I don't think I could let you go now, even if I wanted to."

Lauren felt her own smile matching his. She reached out and took his hand, giving it a gentle squeeze. "I don't want you to let me go."

Rex stood up, pulling her out of her seat. Grinning, Lauren let him, tilting her head up for the kiss she knew was coming.

"Uh, Mom, what's for dinner?"

Rex and Lauren pulled away guiltily, grinning at each other. Lauren looked at her son, standing in the doorway. "Um, chicken breasts on the grill and potato packets."

He crossed his arms over his small chest and planted his feet. "Sounds good."

Then he just stood there, and Lauren knew he thought he was protecting her. "Keegan, it's okay. Rex isn't going to hurt me."

"He just said he has PTSD. That's what Dad has."

Lauren sighed and motioned him into the kitchen. She wasn't surprised he had overheard them. He plopped into the chair to her right, his normal spot, and glanced between them.

"Do you want me to step out?" Rex asked.

Lauren shook her head. "No, we need to talk about this. You're right, Keegan, that is what your dad has. But even you can see the difference between Rex and your father. Sam denied having it for a long time, which led to a lot of issues. Rex knows he has this issue and has made an effort to control it. Your father also drank, which exacerbated the flashbacks. Remember?"

Keegan nodded, his eyes still serious and troubled.

"I very rarely drink, Keegan," Rex said, leaning to rest his elbows on the table. "And I understand your concern for your mom's safety. I would be concerned too, if some guy showed up after one date and you found him kissing your mom."

The tips of Keegan's ears turned pink, but he didn't look away from Rex.

"But I promise you, I would cut off my arm before I ever hurt your mother. Or you. Or anyone. I've devoted my career to taking care of people. I know you don't know me, but I care very much for your mother, and I would like to continue to see her. I understand that you're the man of the house, though, so I would like your permission to continue to see her."

Lauren fought not to let her mouth drop open. She would not have expected that from big, imposing Rex. She glanced at her son. Obviously, the request had taken him off guard as well, and his little cheeks went completely pink.

Lauren appreciated what Rex was trying to do, though. They all had trauma, and Rex was trying to wade through Keegan's the best way he could.

Keegan looked down at his hands for a minute, before he finally looked up at Rex. "We can try it for a while, but if you ever even raise your voice at her, I'll make you leave."

Lauren was surprised at the vehemence in the boy's words, but her heart almost burst with pride. He was turning into such a little man.

Rex didn't snort or do anything dismissive, merely reached out his hand to Keegan. They shook on the deal, and Lauren couldn't help but smile. Rex had done this exactly the way it had needed done.

Keegan stood up from the table and moved to hug her. Lauren took it happily. "Why don't you get a cheese stick to hold you until dinner?"

Keegan moved to the fridge and found a cheese stick. With a last glance between them, he left the kitchen, the dog trailing behind him.

Lauren looked at Rex, shaking her head slightly. "What would you have done if he'd said no?" she asked, curiosity getting the better of her.

"I would have exited stage left," Rex said softly. "He is a part of you, and we need all the parts to fit together for this to work."

Her eyes grew hot, and she had to blink a few times to clear her vision. "Thank you for giving him that respect. We've been to counseling as well, dealing with it from the family side, and that was one of the things that Keegan was the most upset about. That he couldn't do anything about what his father did when he had those flashbacks. Sam never hit me, but there were a few times when I thought I was going to have to fight. And Keegan knew that. I would send him into his room when Sam got that way, or out to play with the dog."

Her voice faded off as she thought about years past. Rex's hand on her own brought her back.

"I meant what I said, though. If I become in any way aggressive, I will remove myself."

Lauren smiled, turning her hand in his. "Have you ever become aggressive to anyone in your life in the past ten years?"

Rex frowned, his mouth pinching tight. "I snapped at my buddy a time or two, but that was usually when he was pushing me to go into counseling. Or lift more weight than I thought my shoulder could take. But overall, no."

Lauren nodded, already knowing the answer. "I don't think Gen would have suggested we go together if she didn't believe in you."

Rex grinned slightly and nodded. "Yeah, she is a pretty good cheerleader. And maybe a decent judge of character."

Reaching out, he took her fingers again. His broad thumb made little circles over her knuckles, and warmth spread through her. There was a look in his eyes, and she knew exactly what he was thinking. She grinned slightly and lifted a brow at him. "I think you know how much I enjoyed earlier."

His mouth tipped up as well. "I think I do. I did as well. In case you didn't realize. When can we do it again?"

It was Lauren's turn to blush, and she grinned. "Well, I don't know. I promised Keegan he could pick something to do this weekend, so it may be a few days."

"Okay," Rex said, nodding. "Well, if something opens up, let me know. Maybe we can go get Mexican or something. I do know this great little place close to downtown."

"That sounds fantastic."

They stood, and it was very easy to step into his arms. She tilted her head up, anticipation sliding through her.

"Oh, excuse me, kids. I was just getting a drink of water," her mother said, striding into the room.

Lauren gave Rex a rolled-eye look, and she could see the laughter in his narrowed eyes. "We'll get back to this," he promised. Then very deliberately gave her a kiss on the lips, before grabbing his bag and heading out of the house.

Lauren gave her mother a peeved look. Sophia grinned slightly and shrugged. "What?"

Lauren shook her head and sighed. "Nothing."

CHAPTER TEN

Rex looked down at the phone and debated answering it. When he'd been on edge last night, he'd called Baylee and Olivia. Neither one of them had answered, which was fine. But now there were messages he needed to respond to from both of them, and Baylee had called several times since.

Sighing, he pressed the touch screen on his radio to answer the call, then started looking for a place to pull over. This would take a few minutes.

"Hey, Bay."

"Rex! Where the heck have you been? I've been calling you!"

"I know," he sighed, pulling into a gas station parking lot. It was busy, but he could park around the side where there wasn't as much traffic. "I was... distracted."

"Are you okay now? You sounded distraught."

Yeah, he probably had. "I'm okay now," he said, and he realized it was true. Seeing that veteran's absolute despair had been hard, but he was more objective about it now. His empathy made him a great nurse, but sometimes it also worked against him. "I'm sorry if I worried you."

"You really did, you butthole. I was on overtime when you called, and my phone was in the locker."

Baylee was a pediatric oncology nurse at Dell Children's Pavilion Austin, and he knew how over-worked she was. It seemed like there were never enough nurses to go around, and her specialty had even more challenges. Rex wasn't sure how she did it, dealing with sick children all the time. But then, Baylee had major cajones.

"That's okay. I just had a bad night, and I needed to talk it through."

"Well, I'm glad Olivia helped you out."

Rex winced. He hadn't really wanted to tell anyone about Lauren yet, but he could see where the conversation was going. "Actually, I couldn't get Olivia either. Isn't she helping that firefighter out or something?"

"Oh, yeah. I forgot about that." She paused. "Well, did you work it out yourself, then?"

"No. I called another friend. A newer friend."

"Oh," she singsonged, her voice rising and lifting. "Anybody I need to know about?"

"Well," he said, squinting into the fading sunlight through the windshield. "Like I said, she's a new friend. Actually, Gen set us up on a date the other night, and we kind of clicked. She was the cop from the robbery I told you about."

"Oh," Baylee breathed. "The one who kept you from going to the nuthouse after you got shot."

Rex snorted. Baylee had a brutal way of looking at things. But then, in the job she was in, he couldn't blame her. There was no sugar-coating kids with cancer. "Yes, she did. Her ex had flashbacks and stuff, and she knew what she was seeing."

"So, this is very interesting to me, because you've never told me about any of the women you've ever dated. You've never even mentioned women to Olivia and I. For a while, we thought you were gay, with the way you were going to the gym all the time. And that would have been totally okay, but…"

Rex burst out laughing. "You seriously thought I was gay? Don't you remember catching me with the pretty little Marine in the storage room? Or the woman from the commissary?"

"Of course, I do! It was burning gossip for days on Nightshade. But that was before the attack. We never heard anything after the attack."

Yeah, he probably had been circumspect in that. For a long time, he hadn't wanted to expose himself to women because of the scars down his hips. He didn't want to have to explain how they'd happened or what had led up to it. His ego wouldn't allow it. It was easier to just not talk about it.

As the words went through his mind, he realized how fucked up they were.

"Rex, you okay?" Baylee's voice was soft, and he could see her in his mind's eye. She'd been a good friend to him, and he'd never been completely honest with her.

"Yeah, just thinking." The silence lengthened between them. "Do you still go to counseling?"

Baylee sighed. "Not as much anymore. I got tired of going through all the gory details. I think they were waiting to see regret or remorse for killing those men, even though they'd raped me, but I stand by what I did. The shrink didn't understand. She expected me to be a weepy woman, and that's just not me."

No, she wasn't. The only time Rex had ever seen her cry was when she talked about putting the tourniquet on Olivia's leg, ensuring that it would have to be amputated after they were rescued. Olivia hadn't blamed her, of course. She had thanked her for saving her life, even as she was dealing with her own trauma.

"I'm glad you killed them," he said simply. "I think it was exactly what you needed to do to get your mind on the right path."

"Yeah," she said, sighing again. "That's what the Delta guys told me."

"Well," he admitted, wondering if he was going crazy. Was he really going to tell her? "I'm glad for more personal reasons."

"What do you mean?" she asked, voice low.

Rex clenched his jaw. Baylee was one of his best friends, and Olivia too, but he'd never told them what had happened to him in that surgery. Compared to what she'd gone through, it was nothing, really. Just an emasculation that he didn't want to admit.

Rex glanced around. It was a sunny afternoon, and people were moving around, going on with their lives. It seemed weird to be talking about this here.

"They almost got me, as well," he admitted, voice low.

There was an audible gasp on the other end of the line. "No…" she breathed. "The same men?"

"Well, the same group. I don't think it was the same men that you killed. I think the Delta Force crew killed the one who almost got me. He was older and spoke some English. Called me a *bacha* boy. He tied me to a gurney and cut my pants off me. That was when the Deltas broke in and took them out. Their timing was impeccable."

"Rex, I am so sorry. I had no idea. Why didn't you tell us?"

He took a deep breath. "Well, for one thing, nothing really happened. It just almost happened. And after what you and Liv had gone through, it seemed trivial for me to talk about it."

"Rex," she admonished. "It's still something you went through that's obviously traumatized you. I know exactly what you were feeling on that gurney."

Baylee's voice got a little choked then, and Rex felt like an asshole for making her talk about it. "I'm.."

"Stop," she said, cutting him off. "Don't you dare apologize. It happened and we're both dealing with it the best way we can. Right? But that feeling of helplessness… It infuriated me, and terrified me, and pissed me off more than I can tell you."

"Yes," he murmured, nodding even though she couldn't see him. "I had shoved it to the back of my mind until EMS tried to strap me down the night of the robbery. I kind of went nuts. But Lauren backed them off and let me come around on my own time."

"It sounds like she has a good head on her shoulders. And maybe a good heart."

He snorted slightly. "I think it's yes to both," he murmured.

The intonation in his voice must have told her something, because she laughed lightly. "Rex, did you sleep with this woman?"

"I did," he confirmed. "And it was… epic."

"You guys suck," Baylee growled, but he could hear the laughter and envy in her voice. "I think that's how Olivia feels about her firefighter."

"If it is, then I wish her all the happiness."

"Yes, I agree," Baylee whispered. "So, you have scars from what this guy did? I knew you were injured, but I thought it was shrapnel, or something."

"No, he cut my scrubs along my hips. Truck got me back together and bandaged up. Then I had stitches when I got to Germany."

"Did she notice the scars?"

Rex frowned, looking out the side window. "She did, but she has enough tact not to dig. That's what I appreciate about her."

"It got you thinking, though. Huh?"

"Yes. And I kind of wanted to get your opinion on what I should say. Because I'm not going to lie, it's very emasculating for me."

Baylee hummed on the other end of the line. "I can see you feeling that way, but you shouldn't. The Taliban were abusers then and they're abusers now. You were shot and beaten, and I'm sure they grabbed you when you were unconscious. Right?"

"Yes."

"Because they knew that was the only time they would be able to get you. You are a formidable man, Rex, and they knew that. It was why they waited until you were incapacitated and possibly why they targeted you in the first place. You know it's all ego for them, and false masculinity."

Rex thought about that for a minute, and what she said made sense. Their entire culture was built on suppression and domination of the weak.

"Thanks, Baylee. I appreciate you talking to me about this."

"Of course, you big goof. I love you. And I only

want the best for you. Talk to her about what happened, be honest, but I have a feeling it won't make a difference to her."

"Okay. I will. Are you doing okay? It's been a while since we talked."

"Yeah," she sighed. "I'm fine. Just getting through the week, you know? That might be why it's gurgling up, too. Because of the anniversary. Do you believe it's been ten years?"

"No," he said, voice clipped. "It really doesn't seem like it's been that long. And you're right. The anniversary has been weighing on me."

"Yeah, me too. But we'll make it through it, Rex. Be honest with her."

"Will do, Baylee. Thanks."

"Of course!"

They hung up then, and Rex smiled at the phone. He felt better about the situation. It wasn't perfect, but what situation was? And if he and Lauren moved forward, she deserved to know what he was dealing with.

It was a little ridiculous the way she kept checking her phone. Even Diego commented on it. "You waitin' on a call or something?"

"No," Lauren sighed, and slipped it into her pocket.

Rex was at work now and if he was as busy as she had been tonight, he may not get a chance to call her for a while. A lot had happened, though, and she wanted to make sure he was okay. And they were okay.

She never would have dreamed that Keegan would stand up for them that way, but it made her mama heart proud. When she and Sam had been going through their divorce, she'd made sure that Keegan wasn't exposed to any of the details. Only what she told him herself. She'd even put a gag order on her mother, because Mom's favorite pastime used to be complaining about Sam. And Lauren hadn't wanted to deal with the fallout of anything he overheard.

Keegan knew very little of what Sam had done, but what he knew was bad enough. Lauren wished that Sam hadn't turned out to be such a stubborn asshole. If he'd only gone for help, they might be in a very different situation.

Now she had a twelve-year-old son without a father. And whether he realized it or not, Keegan needed a strong male figure in his life. It was interesting the way he'd responded to Rex. Not challenging, exactly, but he'd definitely stood his ground.

And Rex had given him the respect the child needed. It had been heartwarming to watch the interaction.

"So, I had a little bird whisper in my ear that they'd seen Chewy," Diego said, glancing at her.

That sharpened Lauren's attention. "Seriously? Where?"

"Down south in the Mission district. I already talked to the sergeant. If we get a quiet minute, we can slide down there and follow up."

Lauren nodded. "That's excellent."

Two hours later, they had a gap in calls. Diego radioed Sergeant Parker and they headed into the Mission district. It was a beautiful area, but not Chew's normal stomping grounds.

"Why down here," Lauren wondered out loud.

"Supposedly, he met a girl, and her family lives down here."

Lauren stared at him incredulously, and Diego nodded at her.

"Okay, well, let's see what we see."

They slid into a residential neighborhood and parked a couple of houses down from the one they were looking for, then they watched. There were two vehicles in the drive, but no one was moving outside. They made note of the plates to give to the detectives.

"So, who is the girl?" she asked.

Diego shook his head. "Didn't recognize the name when I heard it. Maria Henderson."

Lauren shook her head, chewing her lip. It wasn't one she recognized, either. They probably hadn't had any dealings with her.

"This is a pretty decent neighborhood. I can't imagine Chew trading up to this."

Diego shrugged his big shoulders. "It's hard to tell."

They sat in silence, and Lauren hoped there would be some movement before they were sent on another call. After fifteen minutes, her patience was growing thin. "I could just go knock on the door and see what I can find out."

She could tell Diego was thinking about it. She would defer to whatever he thought they should do. Chew was considered armed and dangerous, and they were only supposed to watch for movement. If she could provoke some movement, though…

"Do you have the girl's number?"

Diego shook his head, but he pulled out his phone. "Let me message someone."

They waited another ten minutes for a response. Diego flashed her the number on the screen, and they shared a look. Lauren pulled her own phone out and dialed the number, then she put the call on speakerphone so that Diego could hear.

A female voice answered, hesitant. "Hello?"

"Hello, Maria. This is Officer Cross with the SAPD. We're looking for Larson Charles, also known as Chew or Chewy. We heard through the grapevine that you've been seeing him."

The girl swallowed audibly. "I, I... haven't s-seen him for a while."

That was obviously a lie, but she let it roll. "Okay, Maria. When did you last see him?"

"A few days ago," she said, her voice stronger. "And we're not really together."

She was trying to put distance between the two of them.

"Do you know why we're looking for him?"

Chew was all about ego. If he was trying to show off for her, he may have told her what he'd done. But if he actually liked the girl, maybe he hadn't.

Maria cleared her throat, and Lauren could hear how nervous she was. "Um, no, he didn't."

Lauren glanced at Diego, and he gave her a nod.

"Maria, he's wanted for aggravated assault with a

deadly weapon. He robbed a convenience store, and when the owner wouldn't give him money, he shot him in the stomach."

Maria gasped on the other end of the line and immediately started to cry.

"After he shot Mr. Ahmed, he shot another customer. Both men lived, but if the second man hadn't been a nurse, Mr. Ahmed would have died. And Chew would have a murder warrant."

Maria continued to sniffle on the other end of the line, and Lauren was afraid she would hang up.

"Maria," she called.

"Yes, ma'am," she answered, sniffing.

"We need to find him. He's been on the run for weeks. We're not going to stop. If you know where he is, you need to tell us. And I sincerely hope you're not housing him, because that would make you an accessory."

"I'm not," Maria said quickly. "I swear. And I really haven't seen him for a few days."

"Where has he been staying, Maria?"

"I don't know. He comes by every once in a while to get a shower and some food. I think he's been staying on the streets."

Hm. Sounded believable. But there was something in her voice Lauren didn't quite believe. "Well, this is what you need to do, then. Next time he comes around, you call this number, or message it, and we'll respond. You don't want to be tangled up in this, Maria."

"No, ma'am," she agreed, sounding a little more clear. "I had no idea what he'd done. If I see him, I will definitely let you know."

Lauren glanced at Diego. He had the same 'yeah, right' look on his face.

"You do that, Miss Henderson. For your own sake."

Lauren hung up the phone. "Well, I think she was shocked at the charges, but I'm sure she thinks she's in love and there's some reasonable explanation. She's going to pick up charges herself for this."

Diego frowned and nodded. "Yup. I agree. Let's wait a few minutes and see what happens."

"If she takes off, we're kind of hard to hide."

Diego shrugged. "It's almost full dark. I don't think she'll recognize the car as long as I stay back."

Diego was right. Within just a few minutes, a dark-haired young woman came out of the house and half-jogged to the rear car, a dark colored Honda. She didn't even glance up the street before she backed out and took off in the opposite direction from where they were parked.

Diego followed her carefully, weaving in and out of traffic like a pro. Lauren called their sergeant and let him know what they were doing, and he cautioned them to keep their distance. If they saw Chew, they were to let him know.

Lauren relayed the information, and Diego nodded. "Definitely. I think she's heading toward Travis Park."

"Blending in with the homeless," Lauren murmured, and Diego nodded.

"Luckily, a cop car cruising the area is nothing new."

They followed Maria to a couple of blocks away from the park. She pulled to the right and parked on the street. Diego cruised on past her very calmly and turned right at the cross street. He immediately turned around and parked, giving them a view of Maria's car. It was a little hard to see because of the dark, but the streetlights helped illuminate the street.

Within just a few minutes, a form materialized out of the darkness and jogged across the street to Maria's car. "There he is," Lauren breathed.

The two stood at the car for less than two minutes, and even from a distance, Lauren could see that the conversation was tense. "I think she's giving him the what-for."

Diego nodded. He'd pulled out his phone and was recording the interaction, though it was kind of hard to see. Occasionally, headlights would flash across the suspects' faces, and they could be identified.

Lauren called the detective in charge of the case and left a voicemail. Hopefully, when she came in in the morning, they would put together a task force to come find Chew. And Lauren had a feeling that little Miss Maria would be charged as well.

Chew waved his hands at Maria and shook his head, then his posture changed. It looked like he was pleading with her. Chew closed the distance between them, and Maria accepted a kiss from him. They embraced, before Maria drew back. It looked like she admonished Chew, but he grinned and turned to jog into the night. Lauren watched him as long as she could, before the dark swallowed him. There was no way they would find him now.

At least the detectives would know where he was, though. And she was sure Rex would appreciate the update.

"Let's get back to work," Diego said, pulling away.

CHAPTER ELEVEN

Rex lifted his brows when he read Lauren's message. Chew was living with the homeless miles away.

He hadn't actually been worried about Chew coming after him. Yes, he was a witness to a violent crime, but he didn't think Chew would compound the trouble he was in by trying to take out a witness. That stretched believability. Besides, they had a second witness. The young black man that had been with Chew that night had promised to testify for a reduced sentence. The prosecutor's office had told him that.

"You okay?" Gen asked, stopping beside him at the break table. He glanced up at her.

"Yeah. Message from Lauren that the kid that

robbed Mr. Ahmed last month is living with the homeless downtown."

"Well, at least they know where he is. Kinda. I can't imagine having to wade through all the homeless down there," Gen said, signing off on a chart she was holding.

Yeah, the situation had really gotten bad. Because of San Antonio's temperate conditions, the homeless weathered in the area year-round, and he knew the cops always struggled with crime in the area. The hospitals struggled as well, and he was very glad he didn't work in the ED, where they cared for them a lot.

It was the perfect environment for a kid to hide. No rules and very little law enforcement.

Detective Mueller called him right after lunch, informing him that they would be sending a team in after Chew, but that he still needed to remain vigilant. Rex wasn't especially worried, but he promised that he would.

He worked his shift and headed to the gym after work to expel some excess energy. Since he'd slept with Lauren, she was all he could think about, and he was in a perpetual state of half-hard readiness. He'd thought about inviting himself over again, but that was rude. She had helped him out when his

PTSD had spiked, and he didn't need to take advantage of that.

As he lifted weights, he couldn't help but think of Lauren's body. How it had felt under his hands, the way she had moaned as he touched her. He'd had plenty of sex with other women, but in that moment, he couldn't think of anyone that even held a candle to Lauren. She had been everything he wanted in a woman- strong, competent, sexy as hell. He'd never felt a connection like he had with her. He'd always been too wrapped up in his work to pursue a relationship, but after meeting Lauren, he couldn't help but wonder what it would be like to have her by his side, day in and day out. To have someone to come home to, someone to share his life with. He was well aware that he worked such crazy hours because he had no life.

Man, that Keegan had his mom's spirit, too. Rex was usually pretty good with kids, but there was a guardedness to Keegan that he would have to be careful of if he continued with his mother.

If. That thought made him pause. The mere suggestion that they may not continue had hollowed out his gut with trepidation. Lauren was an amazing woman, and he couldn't imagine not having her in his life. But what did he have to offer her? There was money in the bank, so he could offer her some security. He didn't think Sophia worked, so Lauren was supporting their little family on her wages as a cop.

His movements paused as he considered himself. Besides money, he felt like he would be a strong support system. He'd never really been in love before, but he felt like this was the beginning. Hell, he was already planning how he could change his life to work around hers. That kind of shift in his thinking had to be significant.

Rex became aware that there was a guy staring at him. He gave him a wave and vacated the machine. "Sorry, buddy. Lost in thought."

"No worries," the guy said, taking his place.

Rex headed to one of the treadmills, but decided he wanted to get out of there altogether. He went to the locker room and grabbed his gear, then left the gym.

His steps slowed as he thought about her parting kiss. The need was there, as strong as his own, even after they'd slept together. It had taken all his will to walk away and get in his truck.

Gen would be laughing at him right now if she could see him. He'd never mooned over a woman before. Picking up the pace, he headed to his truck and threw his gear in.

Lauren knew who it was before she even answered the door. Gen had been suspiciously quiet over the past few days. Probably waiting for the combustion to run its course.

When Lauren opened the door, Gen peered around, her movements exaggerated. "Just checking that you don't have a visitor."

Lauren snorted. "Rex isn't here. He's probably at the gym."

Gen sighed as she let herself in and closed the door. Then she crossed to the coffee pot and helped herself to a cup before sitting at the kitchen table. It was the beginning of her weekend, and Lauren knew her visit was probably one of many. Genevieve Frank had her hands in many pies, and she checked on a lot of people when she had the chance. Mostly elderly that didn't like to go to the doctor or refused care for some reason. Gen had a heart of gold, and Lauren knew everything she did was out of love. She was very lucky to count the woman as a friend.

"So, tell me how your date went," she said, sipping at her cup.

Lauren rolled her eyes. "Isn't this a conflict of interest or something? You're friends with both of us, so you need to be Switzerland."

Gen rolled her dark eyes. "Right. Well, then I

shouldn't tell you that Rex has been moping around for two days, waiting on you to call or text. That phone has been in his hand more than I've ever seen it before, and I know he's not checking sports stats."

Lauren snorted, the detail hitting close to home. She'd been the same way, just waiting for acknowledgement. They texted, of course, but it wasn't enough. Yesterday, they'd talked on the phone for two hours after they'd gotten off work. Keegan had looked at her oddly because she'd barely put it down to tell him goodbye for school.

"The date was perfect," she admitted. "We had good food, and when we weren't ready for the night to end, we went to a bar and shot pool for a while."

Gen pretended to swoon. "Oh, my gosh… I remember when Mike and I were like that. We couldn't get enough of each other, and it was so obvious. Did you kiss?"

Lauren nodded. They'd done much more than that, but she wasn't sure Gen was ready to hear all that. "We did. And it was perfect. And dangerous."

Her eyes widened and she leaned forward in her chair. "Oh, really…"

Lauren needed to cool her off a little. "Then, three mornings ago, he called. He was having a hard time dealing with one of the patients you dealt with that night."

Gen's face fell, and she nodded. "Yeah, I knew he was having a hard time. He usually calls one of his Army buddies."

"I don't think they were available. So, he called me, and I invited him over for breakfast. Then I put his ass to work in the barn. And after we got cleaned up, we slept together."

Lauren shrugged and laughed as Gen's face fell, her mouth dropping open in shock. She hadn't really planned to tell Gen they'd slept together, but it was all right.

Gen's mouth was moving, but it took her a moment to get her thoughts in order. "You and he slept together? But... you just went on the date."

Lauren shrugged, grinning. "It was a hot date. Neither one of us wanted it to end. It was a challenge to go our separate ways. And things happen." She shrugged, smiling, and took a sip of her coffee. "I'm sure it will happen again, too, because that man is something special."

Gen got a knowing look in her eyes. "I thought you two would hit it off."

Lauren nodded. "Keegan wants me to see if he can go hiking with us tomorrow."

Gen blinked. "Keegan does?"

"He's not totally sold on the two of us being together, but he's willing to invite him in. I'm very proud of my son."

Nodding, Gen took another sip of her coffee. "That's so mature of him. And I want you to know, if I had any worries at all about Rex, I never would have suggested you two go out."

"I know," Lauren said, reaching across to rest her hand on Gen's. "You've been an excellent friend, and I think you knew what I needed before I did. Now, what's up with you? Did Mike like his birthday gift?"

Lauren smiled as she listened to Gen talk about her life, but half of her mind was counting down the seconds before she could see Rex again.

* * *

REX GRINNED as he answered the phone. "Hey," he said, and wondered how stupid that sounded. But he was ridiculously happy to hear from Lauren.

"Hey," she responded. "Are you done working out?"

"Yeah," Rex lied, gathering up his things as he walked out the door of the gym. "Just getting done. It's nice to hear your voice."

"It's nice to hear your voice, as well," Lauren said, and he could hear the smile in her words. "I know it hasn't been very long, and the text messages are fine, but talking is much better."

"I agree," he said, slinging his bag over his shoulder and walking along the sidewalk. "Seeing you in person is the best, though. When can we get together again?"

She chuckled a little. "Don't talk to me in that sexy voice, damn it. We can't do *that* for a little while. I'm calling because Keegan wanted me to ask you to go on our hike tomorrow. I know you have to work tonight, but..."

Rex blinked, surprised at the offer. "Keegan asked?"

"Yes."

"Then tell him absolutely," he said, meaning the words. "I would love to. I can sleep when we get back."

"Good," Lauren laughed. "I will. Now, what are you wearing?"

Rex laughed out loud, and he didn't care who saw him being so carefree. "Well, I'm wearing bike shorts and a tank top."

"Oh, I bet the guys in there were drooling."

"Yeah, not," he scoffed. "I've got too many old injuries to impress anyone in there."

"Well, your scars impress me," she murmured. "Though you have too many of them."

Rex snorted. "Well, if it were my choice, I wouldn't have any, obviously."

"Obviously."

"I want to see you, Lauren."

"I want to see you as well. You're welcome to come out…"

Blood surged south, and he had to stop walking. "Is your mother home?"

"No," she said. "She teaches a literacy class at the college on Wednesdays, and Keegan is at school. So, if you'd like to come over and shower before your next workout…"

"Give me twenty minutes," Rex said, striding toward his truck. "Twenty-five. I have to stop at the drugstore."

He hung up on her laughter and pressed the button on his key fob before sliding into his truck.

CHAPTER TWELVE

Lauren stood on the front porch of her house, bare ass naked.

Rex slammed the truck into park and climbed out, but he had to stop as soon as he slid out, resting a hand on the frame. The lust had calmed through the drive, but now it hit hard again. Lauren leaned against one post, one foot crossed over the other and her arms crossed over her tummy. She looked like a Viking warrior, her blond hair curling down over her pink-tipped breasts. Her hips were nicely rounded, with one cocked, drawing his gaze to the tangle of curls between her thighs.

Rex looked around, afraid someone would see her, but there was no one for miles. Shoving away from the truck, he walked toward her, a grin spreading his mouth. The morning sun burnished her skin gold, and she was the most beautiful thing he'd ever seen. He stopped at the bottom of the deck stairs, looking up at her. "You take my breath away," he told her simply.

Lauren grinned, padded down two steps so that she could look him in the eyes and wrapped her arms around his neck. "Maybe I can help you with that. I know CPR."

CPR his ass. She kissed the fuck out of him, stealing even more of his oxygen. He returned the favor, though, cupping her hips and pulling her tight. She moaned, turning her head away, and he took the moment to push her back up the stairs. Then, before she could protest, he leaned down and swung her into his arms.

Lauren laughed, and the pain the strain put on his body was totally worth it. He maneuvered through the house and into her bedroom, dropping her to the mattress. Then he was stripping his own clothes off. He grabbed the condoms he'd stuffed into his pocket, then tossed everything else away.

Her eyes latched onto the condoms. "I'm so glad you brought more than one, because I won't lie, this kitty is hungry. I was fine for years, but as soon as we had sex, I was hooked. You're like catnip."

Rex grinned down at her. "Good! It's only fair. I've been walking around with the hard-on from hell, and let me tell you, scrub pants aren't designed to hide boners."

Lauren laughed, cupping his cheeks in her hands. Her gaze connected with his own, and there was something in her expression that made him pause. "What's wrong, Lauren?"

She swallowed and forced a tremulous smile. "I'm strong, Rex. I've had to be for years. But I'm telling you now, you can hurt me."

Rex felt like he'd been punched in the gut. And her vulnerability made his heart ache. "You have the same power, Lauren. I swear to you, I would never deliberately hurt you. Or Keegan. I'm too invested in this working out."

She nodded slightly, her golden hair spread across the pillow. Then she pulled him down into a kiss, shifting her thighs out to wrap around his hips.

Rex was hard as a rock, and when she moved, she pulled him flush against her body. Naturally, his body searched for her opening, and it took everything in him to pull his hips away. It was too soon.

Rex forced his attention to her. Her breasts were tight against his chest, the nipples hard. Pushing himself down the mattress, he wrapped his mouth around one of the taut peaks. She moaned, grasping his head in her hands, but she didn't push him away. Rex played with her nipples, pressing kisses in a line from one to the other. Then he kissed a line down her belly to her wet curls. Curling his arms beneath her hips, he lifted her to his mouth.

Oh, what sweetness…his taste buds came alive as he tasted her for the first time.

Lauren gasped and shuddered as his lips found her swollen clit. He sucked it between his lips, and her hips bucked. Her knees went wide to give him better access, and Rex took advantage of it. He flicked his tongue around her until she came, shuddering hard in his arms. And just as she was catching her breath, he rolled a condom on and sank himself inside her. They both went still as their bodies reacquainted themselves, then they were rocking together, chasing that sweet release. Rex fought to stay in control as long as he could, but he'd been on edge for days. Within just a few minutes, he was burning with the need for release. Lauren panted against him, clutching at his hips to pull him tighter. Then she gave a low, breathy moan. Her body shuddered and twitched, and then he felt a rush of heat as her body orgasmed again.

Rex let his control go, and the orgasm was right

there, waiting. He let it swallow him under, arching into her hard as he ejaculated. His bones disintegrated and he sagged against her as the pleasure rode his body, rippling through him. It was the only time in his life when he didn't feel constant, nagging pain in his old wounds, and he relished the bliss.

He must have drifted off, because when he opened his eyes, Lauren was stroking his hair back behind his ears.

"I'm sorry I'm heavy," he murmured, pushing up on his arms to look down at her.

Lauren merely smiled at him and shook her head slightly. "You weren't. I enjoy holding you."

Rex still pulled away. He had the condom to dispose of. He took care of that, rinsed his hands and returned to the bed. Lauren was on her side, smiling at him slightly. She watched his body move, and he loved the look in her eyes. When he settled onto the mattress beside her, she reached out to touch him, stroking his chest. Her fingers danced over the bullet scar left on his stomach. It was still pink and a little puckered. There was a matching one a few inches around his back, where it had exited. That one was a little larger.

"Does it still hurt?"

"It aches. Especially after a long day. I try to just power through it."

She ran her fingers over the scar on his left shoulder. "And this one?"

He grimaced. "It went through the muscle, and it never healed quite right. It will never be as strong as my right."

"This was a gunshot wound, right?"

Rex took a deep breath, knowing that they needed to talk about it at some point, and now was as good as any. "Yes. When the Taliban overran Nightshade, they shot almost all of our patients. Men on gurneys were killed right and left."

Lauren frowned, and he wondered if this would be too much for her. Yes, she dealt with the criminal side of life, but he was sure she'd never seen anything like what he had in his lifetime.

"They kept the medical personnel alive," he continued, "then brought in soldiers to torture. We had to patch them up so that the Taliban could torture them more. Anyway, they started to take one of the nurses, and I knew what they were going to do. I stood up and one of the guys shot me through the shoulder. Well, I was pissed and I kept coming at them. The next one took me in the thigh."

He pushed the sheets back and showed her his

left thigh. There was a large, circular scar high up near his hip. She ran her hands over it very carefully. "This one looks worse."

"Much," he agreed. "I'm amazed they didn't just kill me. Olivia had to dig the bullet out with forceps. A few pieces splintered off, though. I got an x-ray a few years ago and you can still see a couple of shards of metal."

Lauren shook her head, and her hand drifted down to the puckered line running the length of his thigh and flank. "And this one?"

Rex didn't jerk away, but it was only because he was so relaxed. He stared at Lauren for several long seconds, and she must have understood that these lines were different. She tugged the sheet up over the marks and up his abdomen. "No worries," she smiled, but he could see the hurt in her eyes. "You've bared enough for me tonight."

A week ago, Rex would have accepted the dodge and gone about his life. He was trying to be a better man, though, for her, and that meant no secrets.

He took a breath, his heart galloping. "That was where one of the Taliban soldiers used a knife to cut my scrub pants off me, while I was tied to a gurney. If the Delta Force guys hadn't taken control of Nightshade in that exact moment, I would have been fucked, both literally and figuratively." He tried to laugh, but he knew it didn't sound right.

Lauren's mouth dropped into an O of understanding. "The gurney," she murmured.

Rex nodded tightly. "I've been good for several years, but when the EMS guys brought that gurney in, I'm not gonna lie. I kind of wanted to go off."

Lauren ran her hands over his chest, her eyes shadowed with concern. "I'm sorry, Rex. I understand now why you reacted the way you did. I probably would have done the same thing."

He rocked his head on the pillow, looking up at the ceiling. "It was so ridiculous to me that there was even a chance I could be raped. Me," he looked at her as he tapped his heavy chest.

"You were injured and probably suffering from blood loss, though, right? So, they had the advantage."

"Yeah, that's what Baylee said when I called her the other day. She actually was raped, so what happened to me was nothing, really."

Lauren sat up beside him, her bare breasts jostling as she leaned toward him. Even with all the deliciousness in front of him, though, Rex couldn't look away from her fierce gaze. "What happened to you was as significant as what happened to her.

Don't dismiss it just because of some macho bullshit. It was traumatic. Period. You were attacked, repeatedly, shot, beaten. Why would you think you could just brush all that away?"

Emotion tightened his throat as she defended him. He gave her a slight smile. "Thanks, Lauren."

Reaching up, he pulled her down for a kiss. A huge knot of tension released in his chest, and he knew he'd been carrying it for a long time. Ten years, to be exact. He'd gone the counseling route, and the flashbacks and stuff had eased, but maybe he needed to go back for a few sessions.

Lauren was everything he could ever dream of in a woman, and that she hadn't freaked about what had been done to him gave him heart that they could have something permanent.

Rex threw himself into loving her, determined to banish any thoughts that he was less than a man. He knew it was a ridiculous thought, but that was the way his brain cycled.

Eventually, they moved to the shower, and he used the excuse of rubbing her down to explore every nook and cranny of her body. She was delicious. Toned and strong, she had her own fair share of scars. But everything about her entranced him.

And to her credit, Lauren gave him access to

everything. When he asked about a particularly long scar down her thigh, she twisted her lips. "That was thanks to a car crash I was in with Sam. He picked me up from a night out with the girls and I didn't realize he'd been drinking until he skidded off the road. Thankfully, it was before we had Keegan."

She stretched her leg out into the spray of water, turning the scar this way and that, then grinned up at him. She bent her arm and held her right elbow out, showing him a mottled scar. "I got this in a brutal fight with gravel after Burner spooked at the sight of a tree on the trail."

Rex laughed and cupped the back of her elbow to bring it up for a gentle kiss. "You poor thing."

She nodded her head and lifted her brows theatrically. "Right?"

She lifted up on her toes to kiss his lips, then drew back. A finger danced over the vertical scar on his lips. "What's this from?"

"Rifle butt," he answered tightly.

Lauren shook her head, sadness in her eyes, then she pressed a lingering kiss to the mark. Then she flipped him the bird. "Utility knife," she said, pointing to a faint scar running across the knuckle of her finger.

Grinning, Rex brought her hand to his mouth, pressing a kiss to the knuckle.

"The struggles you've been through," he murmured.

Lauren wrapped her arms around his shoulders, looking him in the eye. "You know I would never poke fun at your service and injuries."

Rex wrapped his arms around her hips. "I know. We're just playing, and it's fine. I think I need to lighten up about them a little."

"I agree," she grinned. "And I dare you to think about the origin of your hip scars when I give you the best blowjob you've ever had."

Rex burst out laughing. "I think…"

But that was all the further his words went as she dropped to her knees in front of him, and he lost all thought.

THEY WERE RUNNING out of time. Lauren glanced at the kitchen clock. It was after noon, and they'd been playing all morning. She was dog tired, but she didn't want him to leave. Rex was very quickly becoming an important part of her life.

Rex seemed reluctant as well, lingering over a

cup of coffee as he watched her drink her own coffee. Lauren felt relaxed and satiated, but her body was humming, too. If he nodded his head toward the bedroom, she'd go, happily, even after all the orgasms he'd given her today.

Rex was an amazing man, and she kept looking for the bad, but it just wasn't there. Rex was wired different from any other man she'd ever met, and she wanted to bask in his attention. She thought she'd been in love with Sam, but Rex was stirring feelings she'd never felt before. Need, obviously, and security. He listened to her thoughts and responded in kind. And he had the emotional maturity to understand her point of view. Maybe it was because he was a nurse, and part of his job was listening to his patients.

Rex set his cup down in the sink. "I need to get home. Sleep is calling me, and as long as I'm here with you, that ain't happening."

Lauren laughed and nodded, stepping forward to wrap her arms around his neck, though her stomach ached at the thought of him leaving. "I understand. We'll see you tomorrow at nine. We don't go very far on the hike, and we usually take Max with us."

Rex gave her a single nod, kissing her on the tip of the nose. "I'll be here," he promised.

Lauren squeezed him in a tight hug. "Thank you for today," she said softly.

Rex drew back, scowling. "Don't be thanking me for what we did today. That was mutual, and you know it."

She nodded, letting him go. He watched her for a long moment, then grabbed up his gym bag and headed out the door. He paused for a moment on the porch and glanced back at her like he wanted to say something, then he shook his head and continued on. Lauren's heart ached as she watched him climb into the truck and drive away.

CHAPTER THIRTEEN

That had been close. He'd been about to tell her that he loved her, and that he'd see her in a while. It had been on the tip of his tongue before he'd realized he was about to jump into the deep end of the pool, and he wasn't sure she wanted to swim with him.

Damn, what if he'd told her he loved her and then she'd smiled at him and said thank you, or something else lame? It would have killed him.

The emotion was there, though. At least, he thought it was love. He'd never really been in love. He'd been with a few good women, but none of them stirred him the way Lauren did.

Keegan was the added cherry on the sundae. The kid was cute and interesting, and seemed to have taken to him. He was excited to go hiking with him tomorrow. With them. And he was excited to see him grow and mature.

That was the thing that was most interesting to Rex. He wanted to be with them into the future. The fact that he was looking forward to something other than work was pretty epic.

Rex headed to his sterile apartment and went to bed. He slept like crap, and he wondered if it was because Lauren wasn't there.

After showering, he headed out the door to his truck. Ahmed's son had reopened the gas station a few days after his father had been shot, and after he was out of the woods. It had taken Rex a couple of weeks before he could go back to the scene of the crime, though. After sitting in his truck for three nights in a row, he'd finally gotten pissed enough with himself to go inside the gas station and get his energy drinks. He was a nurse, so the thought of seeing blood on the floor shouldn't have shook him. It was just his damn brain.

Ahmed's son Ibrahim had welcomed Rex like a long-lost brother when he'd finally entered the store a few nights ago. Rex had asked about his father, and Ibrahim had promised him that he would be back in a few weeks. He was doing physical therapy and harassing all the nurses. Rex had laughed, even as he glanced around the store. Everything broken had been repaired, everything stained had been cleaned. There was no mark of the destruction from that night, other than the way his brain was behaving.

Rex had gotten his drinks, allowing Ibrahim to wave him away with a cheerful 'on the house'. Since then, he'd paid, despite Ibrahim's protests. "You have to show your father you can run the store properly and make money."

Ibrahim had agreed, giving him a broad smile, and they had reached an understanding.

He waved at Ibrahim as he walked through the door and headed toward the back coolers. He passed a guy lingering at the pop cooler, the door open. As he passed him, the guy backed up into him.

"Oh, my bad," the kid said, glancing up.

Rex forced a smile, though his heart was suddenly racing in his chest. "No worries."

Turning, he went on to his cooler and grabbed his drinks, though his skin crawled. The night of the robbery, Chew had worn a mask, but Rex had seen his eyes and he'd seen the tattoo on the side of the kid's neck. They matched the man that had just bumped into him.

Was he going to shoot him in the back as he was grabbing his drinks? Rex let the door fall shut and turned to the next aisle, staring sightlessly at the line of potato chips. Out of the corner of his eye, he saw the kid wander away from the cooler and toward the front end of the aisle. He was taking his time, though. Was he waiting to see if Rex recognized him?

Rex reached out and grabbed a random bag of chips, anger burning in him. If he reacted, Rex had a feeling he would be eating a bullet, either here or in the parking lot, and no one would be the wiser. He glanced up. Ibrahim was chatting to the young man, oblivious to the danger he was in.

Rex felt his pockets. Of course, he'd left his phone in the truck. Fuck!

While he was facing Ibrahim, maybe he should go up behind him and grab him... The thought had merit, but he wasn't typically the aggressor in any situation. Something would go wrong.

If he waited until the kid left, he would be ambushed as soon as he walked outside. Ibrahim would be safe, though.

Scenarios raced through his brain, one after another. Even as he watched, the young man turned and went through the front door, holding it open for a young woman to enter. The guy stepped off the curb and turned right, going around the corner of the building.

He was not going to die, tonight!

Without hesitation, he went to the door and locked the deadbolt. He turned to Ibrahim. "Call 911. That was the man who shot your father."

Ibrahim blinked, then fumbled for the cordless phone behind the counter. Rex watched out the glass doors for Chew to return, but he didn't. Ibrahim stuttered into the receiver, then his words stopped. Rex glanced back and was shocked to see a young woman holding a gun pointed at Ibrahim. It was the young woman that Chew had let into the store.

"Hang up," she told him, her voice shaking as much as her hand holding the gun.

She glanced at Rex. "You move over here."

Rex debated his options. It was obvious she wasn't a criminal. Chew had sent her in here to do something. Was she supposed to listen to see what they said after he left? See if they'd recognized him?

He moved slowly away from the door. He still had his snacks and drinks in his arms, and he wondered if he could throw them at her or something. She waved him over in front of the checkout.

"He didn't do what you said he did," the girl said,

staring at Rex. "I heard you say he shot someone. Larson wouldn't do that."

Rex's brows lifted. "Are you sure about that? Where did you get that gun?"

The dark-eyed girl blinked and looked down at the weapon in her hands. "It's for our protection, from the gangs."

Rex frowned, wondering how naïve she was. "He's part of the gangs. You realize that, right?"

The girl shook her head. "No, he's not. He fights against them. His brother was killed in the gangs, and he hates them. He would never join them."

"When he robbed this store, he was with a kid wearing a red bandana."

The girl blinked, and her gun hand lowered a little. "It doesn't mean anything."

Rex shook his head, praying that the cops would be there soon. Even hang-up 911 calls got checked, right?

A hand banged on the glass door of the store. They all looked over to Chew, who was grinning at her. "Shoot him, baby," he called through the glass. "Then we can run away together."

The girl looked back at Rex, and he knew he was running out of time.

He should have told Lauren he loved her.

* * *

Lauren almost didn't answer the phone. She was in the middle of cleaning the horse stall, and she'd left her phone down the aisle. The possibility it was Rex changed her mind.

She let herself out of the stall and found her phone. It was her partner. "Diego, what are you doing?"

Sirens screamed in the background. "Remember Chew's girl? The stupid one?"

"Yeah," she said slowly.

"Well, she has your man at gunpoint at the Quik Stop."

Lauren's blood chilled in her heart. "What?"

"There was a 911 call. The caller stopped talking though, and set the phone down, and now the dispatcher hears a young woman arguing that Chew didn't shoot the owner."

"What the fuck," she breathed. "Maria?"

"I assume so. I'm running hot to get there, but I thought you could call and try to talk to her. I'll be there in two minutes, but the dispatcher thinks Chew is standing outside the store, trying to get her to do something. She hears yelling in the background, but it's muffled."

"I'll call now," Lauren said. "Be safe," and she hung up.

Paging through the recent list of calls, she found Maria's number and hit dial. Her fingers were shaking.

The phone rang for several long rings, then a female voice picked up. "What!" she snapped.

"Maria," Lauren said, forcing calm into her voice. "This isn't the right thing to do. This isn't you."

"What the hell do you know? Other than lies?"

"Larson is leading you down a dangerous path. You know that in your heart. Why are you there right now? Answer me that. What did he tell you to do?"

The girl was breathing quickly on the other end of the line, and Lauren wondered if she was on something. "He said he wanted to see if the guy recognized him. That was all."

Frustration built in Lauren. "That wasn't all. If he recognized him, what was he going to do?"

Maria started to cry. "I don't know."

"Yes, you do know, Maria. He was going to shoot the witness to his crime. But now that you're there, he's going to have you do it so that he gets off scot free. Did you think about that, Maria? Is he standing there, telling you what to do?"

"Yes," she admitted.

Lauren relished this first chink in the girl's armor. Maybe she was getting through to her. "If he loved you, would he do this to you?"

The silence stretched, and she prayed she'd done enough to rescue Rex.

"No," she admitted, and Lauren heard her sigh.

"Maria, give Rex the gun. Then he can protect you from Chew. Do you hear me, Maria?"

"Yes, ma'am."

There was a jostling on the end of the line, and she thought she heard someone yelling, but it was muffled. Then there was a gunshot, a very distinctive sound, then several more gunshots, and the phone disconnected.

"Rex!"

Lauren paced, then she began calling Rex's phone. Did he have it on him? Had he been shot, again? Had Maria flipped and decided she loved Chew more than her freedom?

It was an interminable, heart-attack inducing two minutes later before an unfamiliar number called her line. She answered immediately. "Yes?"

"It's me, babe. I'm okay."

Lauren burst into tears, pacing the barn aisle as

she heard his voice. "What the hell happened," she cried.

Rex cleared his throat, fighting his own emotion. "The girl, whatever you said to her worked, because she started to hand me the gun. Chew was outside the glass and when he saw her do that, he pulled his own gun, but the cops had just pulled in. There was an exchange of gunfire, but Chew... I don't think he made it."

Lauren sniffed, wishing she was there.

"Don't cry, babe. I'm okay. But I need to go. I need to talk to the officers. Is this your partner?"

"Yes, Diego called and told me what the dispatcher heard. We had tracked Maria down the other night, and I had her number, so I called."

"I'm very glad you did, Lauren, because you saved our lives. I have to go."

"I love you," she blurted, and he paused.

"You know, I love you too," he said, voice deep, like he was fighting his own emotion.

"I'll be there in about half an hour," Lauren told him firmly. "The detective will want to talk to me, too."

"Okay, I'll let them know you're coming."

And he hung up.

Lauren raced into the house, the dogs barking at

her heels. Her mother looked up in surprise when she burst through the door. "What's wrong?"

"Rex needs me." She shooed Max inside, and the other two back to the barn. "He was ambushed at the Quik Stop where he was shot. He's fine, I think."

"Are you serious," Sophia cried.

"I'll have to tell you more when I get back, Mom. I have to go."

She ran to her bedroom, got her concealed carry cross-body purse and changed into a pair of jeans. Her t-shirt was good enough. Then she stuffed her wallet in the purse and darted out the door.

It was the longest forty minutes of her life, getting to that damn convenience store. Traffic had been bad. She had to park down the street because the store itself had been encircled in yellow police tape. Lauren locked her truck and jogged toward the scene.

The coroner van was front and center, and it saddened her that Chew had chosen the route he had.

She found Diego first. He was leaning against the hood of his cruiser, with his arms crossed. Their lieutenant was there, and the two men were talking softly. Lauren crossed to her partner. "You okay, buddy?"

Diego turned and gave her a small, sad smile. "I'm okay, kid."

She reached out and gave him a hug, and he squeezed her tight. Diego had been on the job close to twenty-five years, but he'd never shot anyone in the line of duty. When she drew back, she rested a hand on his shoulder. "Do you want me to call Sharon?"

He shook his head. "I sent her a text. Told her I was all right, but that we'd be tied up for a while. You go on. Your man's inside, comforting the girl, I think."

With a nod, Lauren headed in that direction. Then she realized she couldn't get through. The front door area had been blocked off as the crime scene techs gathered evidence. There was a sheet-draped body laying across the entry. Diego's service weapon had already been collected, and he would have to talk to the detectives before he could do anything else. When there was an officer involved shooting, the officer had to jump through several hoops to clear them of all wrong doing. Gunfire was the very last option they ever wanted.

Lauren could see Rex through the glass, but traffic was going in and out through the back door. She circled through the alley and went into the Quik

Stop storage room, then through the door to the store. Rex was crouched down beside a handcuffed, weeping girl, one hand resting on her quaking shoulder. When Lauren entered his line of sight, a curious expression crossed his face, like he couldn't believe she was there. He pushed to his feet, grimacing from being in the crouch, and met her halfway. His huge arms wrapped around her, almost squeezing the breath from her. "You're here," he breathed.

That was when she felt the quiver in his muscles. He'd been caring for the girl, but now that Lauren was here, he could loosen his hold on his emotions a little. Lauren held him tight, nuzzling kisses into his neck and telling him he was all right.

Eventually, the quakes eased and she loosened her hold. She didn't let him go, though. Instead, she leaned back in his arms and looked up into his face. "You're going to have to find a new snack store."

In spite of the dire situation, he chuckled, pressing a kiss to her temple. "I think I agree," he said softly.

Detective Mueller came over to them, then, and Lauren knew they had to be interviewed. Probably separately. A death had occurred, and they were all involved.

Shelly was no-nonsense when she interviewed Lauren. It helped that Lauren had an app on her phone that recorded calls. She sent Detective Mueller a copy of the recording, and Shelly finally smiled and let her go.

Then it was Rex's turn for the interrogation. They stepped off to a corner, and Shelly asked him questions for several minutes. When he returned, Shelly nodded at them both. "You may leave the scene. I'll call you if I have more questions."

Rex glanced at Maria. "What's going to happen to her?"

"Well, even though she's upset, she still committed a crime. It's assault at the very least, if not accessory to aggravated assault with a deadly weapon for the original robbery."

Rex shook his head. "I don't want to press charges, if that means anything. I don't think she realized what she was doing."

Shelly gave a single nod. "I'll put it in my report, but it's ultimately up to the prosecutor's office."

They walked through the back room of the store and through the door into the cool night air. Rex walked out into the parking lot for a few minutes, just breathing, and Lauren didn't blame him. He'd been through a traumatic experience, and he needed to deal with it however he could. She stood to the side and let him take his time.

Eventually, he turned to her. "Think we can go get some fur therapy?"

"Absolutely," she said, and led him wide around the melee of cop cars, ambulances, and fire. Neither one of them looked at the front of the store.

* * *

REX CALLED Gen and told her what had happened, and that he wouldn't be in that night. She understood and promised to call him later. Then he sank back in the truck seat and turned to watch Lauren drive. He would have to get his truck later, but it wasn't a priority.

Lauren looked like she'd been in the barn. "Do you think the animals are still awake? Do they sleep at night like we do?"

Lauren gave him a smile, her face lit by the dash lights. "They sleep, but they will always wake up for treats."

And that's exactly what they did. Rex moved from stall to stall, doling out treats. Then he sat on a hay bale, rubbing Winnie's thick fur while Lauren finished up. Lauren flicked off the lights, then sat with him on the bale, listening to the animals settle in for the night.

"You know what was going through my head tonight?" he murmured.

"What," she said softly.

"I was kicking myself in the ass because I hadn't told you I loved you earlier. When I left."

She chuckled lightly, taking his hand in her own. "I was struggling with the same thoughts."

He glanced at her, and there was just enough light from the security light outside to see his face. "Isn't it too soon? I mean, we barely know each other."

Lauren shrugged. "I don't think it matters, sometimes. You see a person and they excite you and challenge you, and they fit in your life like they were meant to be there. I looked at you across the breakfast table and it felt right. Yes, it's soon, but we have time to get to know each other better."

"I still want to go on the hike in the morning. And any other outings Keegan wants to do. He's such a cool kid. I want to be there for him, too."

Tears filled her eyes. He had just reaffirmed what she'd told him. "I don't care if it's early or not. I love you, Rex Neptune. And with the way you get into trouble, I think it's important to tell you every chance I get."

Rex laughed and pulled her up over his lap. "I love you, Lauren Collins. Ever make love on a hay bale before?"

She laughed, snugging her hips down tight to his own. "No, but you should know, Mom has been looking out the window and waiting for us to come in. She wants to check on you, as well."

Rex sighed, running his hands up beneath her t-shirt to cup her breasts. "Will she overlook me spending the night?"

"I think she will. Let's go in."

Rex stood up from the bale, his hands cupped under her ass. Lauren giggled and wiggled free, and they walked across the driveway.

EPILOGUE

EPILOGUE

3 weeks later…

"He looks like a sack of potatoes," Keegan said, snorting with laughter.

Lauren turned in the saddle to watch Rex bounce awkwardly up the hill. He was riding Missy, the gray mare, and the gentlest horse they had. The rider didn't really need to do anything other than sit in the saddle, but Rex didn't understand that yet. He was hunched over the horn and seemed a little crooked in the saddle.

In his defense, Rex was the biggest person riding the smallest horse. She'd bought Missy for Keegan when he was learning to ride. Once he'd gotten proficient, she'd bought him Ranger, a peppy little gelding that he could grow into. Missy was still a good horse, though, and perfect for novices.

Burner, her horse, would suit Rex's size better, but she didn't trust Burner not to go tearing through the desert with him.

"Jeez, he does look like a sack of potatoes, doesn't he," she laughed.

The three of them had been riding a couple of times. Rex had admitted that he'd always wanted to learn, and that since she and Keegan enjoyed it, he *needed* to learn. So, they'd started riding and camping on the weekends, and it filled her heart with love that he wanted to be with them that way.

They'd put the Quik Stop in their history, and they were moving forward with their relationship. All in, as he said.

"I know you guys are laughing at me," he grumped as he crested the hill and Missy stopped beside them.

Lauren jumped down to the ground and handed her reins to Keegan to hold, then she went to Rex, resting a hand on his leg. "Hold on," she warned, before she pushed on the saddle to straighten it on Missy's back. "Now," she whispered, glancing over at Keegan. The boy was leaning down and adjusting his stirrup, not paying attention to them. "You need to loosen your hips like you're making love."

Rex's mouth tipped up in a smile, his ocean blue eyes twinkling under the new cowboy hat she'd gotten him. "Oh, really."

Lauren nodded. "I won't get jealous. I promise."

Rex leaned over further, dropping a kiss to her mouth. "I'll try that, babe. I love you."

"I love you."

Gen told them it was disgusting how in love they were, but Lauren didn't care. She'd found more happiness than she ever could have expected.

And Rex seemed more grounded as well. He'd cut back on his hours a little to be with them more, and he'd moved into the house full-time. Sophia had lifted her brows, but when she'd seen how happy they were together, she didn't protest.

Lauren returned to Burner and stepped into the saddle. "Let's go a little further."

She took off in a trot and glanced back. Rex was doing much better staying in the saddle. He gave her a wink and a grin, and her heart expanded with love just a little more.

THE END...

About JM…

NY TIMES and USA Today Bestselling author J.M. Madden writes compelling romances between 'combat modified' military men and the women who love them, but occasionally she writes spicy, angst-ridden love. An eternal optimist, she believes there is a soulmate for everyone, no matter what the situation or physical challenge.

KEEP YOUR HEAD UP AND YOUR HEART STRONG!

✔WWW.JMMADDEN.COM

✔My FB Like page- https://www.facebook.com/JMMadden58

✔Sign up for my Newsletter if you haven't already. You get 4 free books!

✔Follow me on Instagram- https://www.instagram.com/jm_madden_58/

✔The Lost and Found Series Discussion Group-https://www.facebook.com/groups/433871413415527

✔Tiktok-	https://www.tiktok.com/@author-jmmadden

OR you can email me at authorjmmadden@gmail.com

ALSO-

If you love the book, **PLEASE** leave a review! We really do notice a difference when readers support us!

Thank you so much!

JM

OTHER BOOKS BY JM MADDEN

Reclaiming The SEAL

Loving Lilly

Her Secret Wish

Mistletoe Mischief

Lost and Found Pieces

Lost and Found Pieces II

<u>Twilight Dreams</u>

A Warrior to Love

Slow Burn

The Embattled Road

<u>The Lowells of Honeywell, Texas</u>

Forget Me Not

Untying his Not

Naughty by Nature

Trying the Knot

<u>The Lost and Found Series had several spinoffs-</u>

If you love dogs and would like to read about a concierge service helping military personnel out of difficult spots, check out the **Helping Hands, Healing Hearts** Series.

Healing Home

Wicked Healing

Healing Hope

If you like a paranormal twist to your military, check out the **Dogs of War**! (If you love Christine Feehan's Ghost Walkers you should enjoy this series!)

Genesis

Chaos

Destruction

Retribution

Catalyst

If you would like to read a Navy SEAL book with older characters, check out:

SEAL Hard

Flat Line

Shadow of the Moon

Shadow Games

Standalone books by J.M. Madden

A Touch of Fae

Second Time Around

A Needful Heart

Wet Dream

Love on the Line

The Billionaire's Secret Obsession

The Awakening Society Box Set

There are many more books in this fan fiction world than listed here, for an up-to-date list go to www.AcesPress.com

You can also visit our Amazon page at:
http://www.amazon.com/author/operationalpha

Special Forces: Operation Alpha World

Christie Adams: Charity's Heart

Linzi Baxter: Dangerous Rescue

Misha Blake: Flash

Anna Blakely: Rescuing Gracelynn

Julia Bright: Saving Lorelei

Cara Carnes: Protecting Mari

Kendra Mei Chailyn: Beast

Melissa Kay Clarke: Rescuing Annabeth

Gia Cobie: Saved from Revenge

Samantha A. Cole: Handling Haven

KaLyn Cooper: Spring Unveiled

Janie Crouch: Storm

Jordan Dane: Redemption for Avery

Tarina Deaton: Found in the Lost

Riley Edwards: Protecting Olivia

Dorothy Ewels: Knight's Queen

Lila Ferrari: Protecting Joy

Nicole Flockton: Protecting Maria

TL Reeve and Michele Ryan: Extracting Mateo
Ariana Rose: Chasing Paige
Deanna L. Rowley: Saving Veronica
Angela Rush: Charlotte
Rose Smith: Saving Satin
Tyler Anne Snell: Cowboy Heat
Lynne St. James: SEAL's Spitfire
E.M. Shue: Discovering Tyler
Bella Stone: Rexar
Jen Talty: Burning Desire
Reina Torres, Rescuing Hi'ilani
LJ Vickery: Circus Comes to Town
R. C. Wynne: Shadows Renewed

Delta Team Three Series
Lori Ryan: Nori's Delta
Becca Jameson: Destiny's Delta
Lynne St James, Gwen's Delta
Elle James: Ivy's Delta
Riley Edwards: Hope's Delta

Police and Fire: Operation Alpha World
Freya Barker: Burning for Autumn
B.P. Beth: Scott
Jane Blythe: Salvaging Marigold
Julia Bright, Justice for Amber

Gia Cobie: Saved from Revenge
Hadley Finn: Exton
Emily Gray: Shelter for Allegra
Danielle M. Haas: Crossroads of Betrayal
Deanndra Hall: Shelter for Sharla
Jenna Harte: Dead But Not Forgotten
Amber Kuhlman: Protecting Paisley
Reina Torres: Justice for Sloane
Aubree Valentine, Justice for Danielle
Maddie Wade: Finding English

Tarpley VFD Series
Silver James, Fighting for Elena
Deanndra Hall, Fighting for Carly
Haven Rose, Fighting for Calliope
MJ Nightingale, Fighting for Jemma
TL Reeve, Fighting for Brittney
Nicole Flockton, Fighting for Nadia

As you know, this book included at least one character from Susan Stoker's books. To check out more, see below.

SEAL Team Hawaii Series

Finding Elodie
Finding Lexie
Finding Kenna
Finding Monica
Finding Carly
Finding Ashlyn
Finding Jodelle

Eagle Point Search & Rescue

Searching for Lilly
Searching for Elsie
Searching for Bristol
Searching for Caryn
Searching for Finley (Sept 2023)
Searching for Heather (Jan 2024)
Searching for Khloe (May 2024)

The Refuge Series

Deserving Alaska
Deserving Henley

Deserving Reese

Deserving Cora (Nov 2023)

Deserving Lara (Feb 2024)

Deserving Maisy (TBA)

Deserving Ryleigh (TBA)

Delta Team Two Series

Shielding Gillian

Shielding Kinley

Shielding Aspen

Shielding Jayme (novella)

Shielding Riley

Shielding Devyn

Shielding Ember

Shielding Sierra

SEAL of Protection: Legacy Series

Securing Caite (FREE!)

Securing Brenae (novella)

Securing Sidney

Securing Piper

Securing Zoey

Securing Avery

Securing Kalee

Securing Jane

Delta Force Heroes Series

Rescuing Rayne (FREE!)

Rescuing Aimee (novella)

Rescuing Emily

Rescuing Harley

Marrying Emily (novella)

Rescuing Kassie

Rescuing Bryn

Rescuing Casey

Rescuing Sadie (novella)

Rescuing Wendy

Rescuing Mary

Rescuing Macie (novella)

Rescuing Annie

Badge of Honor: Texas Heroes Series

Justice for Mackenzie (FREE!)

Justice for Mickie

Justice for Corrie

Justice for Laine (novella)

Shelter for Elizabeth

Justice for Boone

Shelter for Adeline

Shelter for Sophie

Justice for Erin

Justice for Milena

Shelter for Blythe
Justice for Hope
Shelter for Quinn
Shelter for Koren
Shelter for Penelope

SEAL of Protection Series

Protecting Caroline (FREE!)
Protecting Alabama
Protecting Fiona
Marrying Caroline (novella)
Protecting Summer
Protecting Cheyenne
Protecting Jessyka
Protecting Julie (novella)
Protecting Melody
Protecting the Future
Protecting Kiera (novella)
Protecting Alabama's Kids (novella)
Protecting Dakota

New York Times, USA Today and *Wall Street Journal* Bestselling Author Susan Stoker has a heart as big as the state of Tennessee where she lives, but this all American girl has also spent the last fourteen years living in Missouri, California, Colorado, Indiana, and Texas. She's married to a retired Army man who now gets to follow *her* around the country.

www.stokeraces.com
www.AcesPress.com
susan@stokeraces.com

Made in the USA
Coppell, TX
25 July 2023

19551165R20134